Olivia
Adams

Also by Rebecca Stead

When You Reach Me

REBECCA STEAD

Andersen Press • London

This edition first published in 2013 by
Andersen Press Limited
20 Vauxhall Bridge Road
London SW1V 2SA
www.andersenpress.co.uk

4 6 8 10 9 7 5

First published in 2012 in the United Kingdom by Andersen Press Limited

First published in 2012 in the United States of America by
Wendy Lamb Books, Random House Children's Books
Random House, Inc.
New York

British Library Cataloguing in Publication Data available.

ISBN 978 1 84939 542 7

Printed and bound in Great Britain by
Clays Limited, Bungay, Suffolk, NR35 1ED

For Randi

The Science Unit of Destiny

There's this totally false map of the human tongue. It's supposed to show where we taste different things, like salty on the side of the tongue, sweet in the front, bitter in the back. Some guy drew it a hundred years ago, and people have been forcing kids to memorize it ever since.

But it's wrong—*all* wrong. As in, not even the slightest bit right. It turns out that our taste buds are all alike, they can taste everything, and they're all over the place. Mr. Landau, seventh-grade science teacher, has unrolled a beaten-up poster of the ignorant tongue map, and he's explaining about how people have misunderstood the science of taste since the beginning of time.

Everyone in my class, even Bob English Who Draws, is paying attention today, because this is the first day of "How We Taste," also known as The Science Unit of Destiny. They all believe that sometime in the next ten school days, at least one person in the room is going to discover his or her own personal fate: true love or tragic death.

Yes, those are the only two choices.

1

Bob English Who Draws is really named Robert English. Back in fourth grade, our teacher, Ms. Diamatis, started calling him Bob English Who Draws because he was always zoning out and doodling with a superfine Sharpie. Ms. Diamatis would say, "Bob English Who Draws, can you please take us through the eights?" It was her job to make sure no one got out of fourth grade without lightning-fast multiplication skills. And everyone has called him that ever since.

While the rest of the class is hanging on every syllable that comes out of Mr. Landau's mouth, I'm looking at the false tongue poster and I'm kind of wishing it *wasn't* wrong. There's something nice about those thick black arrows: sour here, salty there, like there's a right place for everything. Instead of the total confusion the human tongue actually turns out to be.

People, People

It's Friday afternoon, last period. Gym. Ms. Warner and I have done our Friday high five. We do it every week, because I hate school and she hates work, and we both live for Friday.

We're playing volleyball, with an exclamation point. Ms. Warner has written it on the whiteboard outside the gym doors: *Volleyball!*

The combination of seeing that word and breathing the smell of the first floor, which is the smell of the cafeteria after lunch, creates some kind of echo in my head, like a faraway shout.

In the morning, the cafeteria smells fried and sweet, like fish sticks and cookies. But after lunch, it's different. There's more kid sweat and garbage mixed in, I guess. Or maybe it's just that, after lunch, the cafeteria doesn't have the smell of things to come. It's the smell of what has been.

Volleyball!

Ms. Warner is at the net with her hands on her knees,

calling stuff out to kids and smiling like crazy. "Shazam!" she yells when Eliza Donan gives the ball a halfhearted bump with her forearm. "Sweet shot!"

If you didn't know Ms. Warner, you'd think there's no place she'd rather be. Maybe she's trying out my mom's famous theory that if you smile for no reason at all you will actually start to feel happy. Mom's always telling me to smile and hoping I'll turn into a smiley person, which, to be honest, is kind of annoying. But I know she's extra-sensitive about me ever since she and Dad made their big announcement that we had to sell our house. She even recorded a bunch of *America's Funniest Home Videos* for me to watch: my smile therapy.

I tell Mom to please save her miracle cures for the hospital. She's a nurse in the intensive-care ward, where she has to check on her patients every fifteen minutes. It's a hard habit to break, I guess, all that checking. I've been watching the shows, though, and they do make me laugh. How can you not laugh at *America's Funniest Home Videos*? All those wacky animals. All that falling down.

I count the number of rotations we have left in "Volleyball!" before it's my serve and then glance at the huge clock in its protective cage on the wall. I calculate a fifty-fifty chance that the dismissal bell will save me, but the next thing I know I'm in that back corner, balancing the ball on one palm and getting ready to slap it with the other.

Don't look at the ball.

Point your eyes where you want the ball to go.

But the advice in my head is useless, because time slows

4

down until everyone's voices transform into something that sounds like underwater whale-singing.

Well, obviously "underwater," I tell myself. Where else are you going to find whales?

I should be paying attention to the ball.

Just as I'm about to smack it, I get this feeling, this premonition, that I'm going to land the ball at least somewhere on the other side of the net, maybe even in that big hole in the second row where Mandy and Gabe are being careful not to stand too close because they secretly like each other.

I'm wrong, though. The ball goes high, falls short, and hits the floor between the feet of Dallas Llewellyn, who is standing right in front of me. My serve is what is called an epic fail, and some of the girls start doing the slow clap.

Clap.

Pause.

Clap.

Pause.

Clap.

It's sarcastic clapping. You know that famous philosophical question "What is the sound of one hand clapping?" Well, I have no idea, but it has to be better than the slow clap.

Ms. Warner is yelling "People! People!" like she always does when kids are mean and she has no idea what to do about it.

Dallas hands me the ball for my second try and I hit it right away, just to get it over with. This time it goes way left, out of bounds. Then the bell rings, kids fly in all directions, and the week is over.

* * *

I stroll over to Ms. Warner, who's sitting on a stack of folded-up mats against the wall, making notes on her clipboard.

"Happy weekend, G!" she says. "We made it. Forty-eight hours of freedom and beauty, looking right at us."

Ms. Warner is trying to make the name G stick to me. My name is Georges, which is pronounced just like "George" because the S is silent, but of course some kids call me "Jor-Jess," or "Gorgeous." I don't much care. There are worse things to be called than Gorgeous, even for a boy.

"G? You in there?" Ms. Warner is waving one hand in front of my face. "I said happy weekend."

"Yeah," I say, but for once I don't want to think about the weekend, because we're moving out of our house on Sunday. Mom will be at the hospital, so I'm Dad's designated helper.

Ms. Warner is smiling at me. "Pop a squat," she says, patting the pile of gym mats. I lie down on the floor instead.

A few of the kids have decided to kick off their weekends by hurling volleyballs at the giant clock. They can't hurt it, because of the wire cage, but Ms. Warner still feels duty-bound to stop them. "Be right back," she tells me, and then she rushes off yelling "People! People!"

Lying down on the floor was a mistake. Lying down suggests I'm dying, and attracts vultures. Or if not dying, defeated. And if not vultures, Dallas Llewellyn.

Dallas is standing over me. Before I can blink, he's got one foot on my stomach. Just resting it there.

"Nice serve, Gorgeous."

This is classic bully crap. That's what Mom called it when she saw the things someone wrote on one of the dividers in my

6

notebook a few weeks ago. I would never have showed them to her, but she goes through my stuff sometimes. "Catching up," she calls it.

Dallas's sneaker is resting on the soft spot right below my solar plexus. It hurts. I do some shallow breathing, because I don't want his heel to puncture any of my internal organs.

"We were losing anyway," I tell him, though I have no idea whether that's true.

"It was *tied*," he snarls, and I try to shrug, which is hard to do when you're lying on your back with someone's foot in your gut. I want to tell him what I know, which is that the fate of the world doesn't hang on whether a bunch of seventh graders win a game of volleyball in some really old school in Brooklyn that smells like a hundred years of lunch.

Instead, I wrap my hands around his ankle, and lift. I've been doing morning weights with Dad for about a year—just these little blue plastic ones that tuck under my parents' bed, but there's a cumulative effect. Dallas circles his arms uselessly and then hits the floor.

It's a harmless bounce. I would never want to hurt him. I know that soon all of this will be a distant memory for both of us. But pain is pain, and I would rather avoid it.

A Boy Your Age

On Sunday morning I stand in the lobby of our apartment building, watching the movers come in and out. Dad says I'm holding the door, but the door is actually propped open with a scratched-up wooden triangle that reminds me of the blocks area in pre-K. What I'm really doing is looking down at that wedge of wood and thinking about how I used to make these super-long car ramps with Jason, and how Jason dresses like a skateboarder now, which he isn't, and how whenever Carter Dixon or Dallas Llewellyn calls me Gorgeous, Jason just stands there.

I lean past the lobby door so I can see up and down the empty sidewalk. It's super-bright out, and the trees make cool shadows on the pavement.

Dad's in the moving truck, making sure the furniture comes out in a certain order. I'm guessing he's being about as helpful as I am, standing guard over my wooden wedge.

I'm hearing a sound. It's a funny, high-pitched buzzing that I think maybe I've *been* hearing for a while, without noticing. There should be a word for that, when you hear something and simultaneously realize that it's been swimming around in your brain for five minutes without your permission.

I glance around to see what's buzzing, first at the ancient yellow chandelier above my head, then at the shiny silver intercom on the wall. It's the kind with a keypad and a little camera that lets the people in their apartments see who's in the lobby before deciding whether to let them in. Dad has already shown me how the whole thing works.

I take a step toward the intercom, and the buzzing stops.

I go back to thinking about Jason, who was my every-day-after-school friend until the end of sixth grade, when he went to sleepaway camp for seven weeks and then started sitting at the cool table in September like he'd been there all along.

All of a sudden there's a whole lot of noise coming from somewhere right above me, a weird mix of rattling, clicking, and pounding that echoes around the tiled lobby, and then two dogs appear on the landing at the top of the stairs, a giant yellow one and a small dark one. There's a boy about my size behind the dogs, holding the twisted leashes in one hand and trying to keep a grip on the banister with the other.

I flatten myself against the open door, thinking the dogs will pull the boy past me and out the front, but they don't. Instead, they drag him almost in a circle, to a door underneath the stairs. They make the turn so fast that he actually hops on one leg for a few seconds, almost tipping over sideways, like in a cartoon.

The door under the stairs is closed. The dogs wait in front of it, wiggling and wagging, while the boy, not once looking at me, struggles to get a huge ring of keys out of his front jeans pocket. He picks a key, unlocks the door, and pushes it open. I can see another set of stairs, going down.

The dogs surge, pulling the boy down the stairs, and the door slams shut behind them. Loudly. And then everything is quiet again.

I know exactly what Dad would say if he were here. He wouldn't mention the weird stuff—how the dogs ran straight to a mystery door under the stairs, or the kid's enormous key ring.

Dad would only say, "Look, Georges! A boy your age."

sir ott

The first thing Dad does is hang the Seurat in our new living room. It's not a real Seurat, because that would make us millionaires. It's a poster from a museum. I feel a little better as soon as I see it on the wall above the couch, exactly where it always was at home. I think we both do.

Two summers ago we went to Chicago, where the real painting takes up one entire wall of the Art Institute. What you can't tell from our poster is that the picture is painted entirely with dots. Tiny little dots. Close up, they just look like blobs of paint. But if you stand back, you see that they make this whole nice park scene, with people walking around in old-fashioned clothes. There's even a monkey on a leash. Mom says that our Seurat poster reminds her to look at the big picture. Like when it hurts to think about selling the house, she tells herself how that bad feeling is just one dot in the giant Seurat painting of our lives.

When I was little, I thought my parents were calling our poster the "Sir Ott," which is how you pronounce *Seurat*, the name of the artist from France who painted the picture. And

I still think of the poster that way—like it's this guy, Sir Ott, who has always lived with us.

In my head, Sir Ott has a kind of personality. Very polite. Very quiet. He watches a lot of television.

Seurat's first name? It was Georges.

Here's a piece of advice you will probably never use: If you want to name your son after Georges Seurat, you *could* call him George, without the S. Just to make his life easier.

After Sir Ott is up on the wall (and perfectly level), Dad and I start with the kitchen stuff, unwrapping dishes and glasses. It's amazing how much work it is to move just twelve blocks.

I'm tossing all the silverware into a drawer until I remember that Dad will probably have a heart attack because he can't stand to see things all jumbled up like that, and so I stop and do it right—forks with forks, tablespoons separate from teaspoons.

We make a good team, and soon we have about ten giant plastic bags stuffed with the crumpled-up newspaper everything was wrapped in.

"Let me show you the basement," Dad says. "That's where the garbage and recycling go." Because the garbage is my job.

At our house, doing the garbage meant wheeling two big plastic bins out to the curb. I could take both at once, steering them in two directions around the crack on the broken concrete path and bringing them back together again on the other side. It's not as easy as it sounds. It's a big crack: I tripped over it when I was five and chipped my front tooth. I imagine the new owners of our house hitting that crack on trash day, their cans tipping and their garbage going everywhere.

Dad and I toss the bags of newspaper into the hall, making a small mountain. When the elevator opens, there's a guy in it, standing next to two big suitcases. He's wearing a baseball cap with a fish on it.

Dad tells him we'll take the next one. "Don't want to drown you," he says, pointing at our massive pile of recycling.

"I appreciate it!" the man calls as the door is closing.

Dad and I watch the beat-up metal arrow on the wall above the elevator move from 3, to 2, then L, for lobby. Dad loves old stuff like that, like the big yellow chandelier downstairs and the tiled hallway floors that will never, ever be clean again. He calls it "faded elegance." That's sort of his job now—he's officially still an architect, but ever since he got laid off last year, he mostly helps people make their new houses look old. Which I think is a little crazy, considering that there are plenty of old houses they could just buy in the first place.

Dad's getting fired has a lot to do with why we sold our house. Mom says it was partly a blessing in disguise because Dad's always talked about starting his own business, and now he's finally done it. So far he only has three customers. Or clients, as he calls them.

The basement has bumpy gray walls and a few lightbulbs hanging down from the ceiling on neon-yellow cords. There's a line of garbage cans against the far wall. Dad and I stack the bags of paper in the recycling area.

Next to the last garbage can, there are two doors. One of them says SUPERINTENDENT. There's a pad taped to it, with a stubby pencil hanging from a string, and a Post-it that says: DATE YOUR WORK REQUESTS.

The second door has something stuck to it too—a piece of loose-leaf paper with words scrawled on it:

Spy Club Meeting—TODAY!

I can't tell how old the paper is, but it's a little curly around the edges.

Dad is studying it. "What a ridiculous sign."

"I know—dumb."

"I mean, how are we supposed to attend the meeting if they don't announce the time?"

"Ha, ha."

"I'm serious." Dad takes the pencil-on-a-string from the superintendent's door and stretches it over to the Spy Club notice. It doesn't quite reach, so he has to write along the very edge of the paper:

WHAT TIME?

When Dad gets an idea into his head, it's no use trying to stop him. So I just watch him do it. Dad writes with these perfectly even block letters. They teach you that at architecture school.

"Can we go now?"

Upstairs, Dad has me flatten a stack of empty boxes while he puts the books on the bookshelves. I catch myself thinking about that Spy Club sign, and how some kid might get excited that someone is actually coming. But that sheet of paper has probably been stuck up there for months. Years, even.

"I should probably take some of these boxes downstairs," I say.

"Want me to come?" Dad is looking at the bookshelves, deep in thought, deciding exactly which book should go where. Once, Mom came home from work and discovered that he had turned all the books around so that the bindings were against the wall and the pages faced out. He said it was calming not to have all those words floating around and "creating static." Mom made him turn them back. She said that it was too hard to find a book when she couldn't read the titles. Then she poured herself a big glass of wine.

"I can handle the basement," I tell Dad. "You finish the books."

Downstairs, I prop the boxes against the wall and glance over at the Spy Club notice.

Under Dad's *WHAT TIME?* something is written in orange marker:

1:30?

Great. Now Dad has gone and raised the hopes of some kid in the building. I stand there for a minute, then stretch the stubby-pencil string over to the paper the way Dad did.

OK, I write.

When I get back upstairs, Dad has a book in each hand and he's just staring, like his life depends on which one he picks. He's surrounded by five boxes, all still full of books. He'll never be done.

"The blue one," I tell him.

He nods and puts it on the shelf. "I was leaning toward the blue." He stands back. "What do you think so far?"

"Looks good. And it's less echoey in here now."

"You want to call Mom at the hospital? We can fill her in, tell her how it's going."

"Maybe later." I don't like the way Mom's voice sounds at the hospital. Tired.

"I need lunch," Dad says. "DeMarco's?"

I say yes to pizza. "But can we make it quick?" I ask. "I have a meeting downstairs at one-thirty, thanks to you."

Dad stares at me for a second and then bursts out laughing. "Seriously? The Spy Club? I was sure that sign was ten years old!"

But of course he loves that I'm going through with it.

"What if it's a seven-year-old or something?" I complain on the way to DeMarco's.

"Only one way to find out," Dad says cheerfully. As if he isn't to blame for the whole situation.

Spy Club

I get to the basement at 1:31 p.m. The Spy Club door is open, just a crack, and there's light coming from inside. I'm holding a little bag of crumpled-up newspaper, for camouflage, in case it *is* a seven-year-old.

I carry my bag down to the last trash can—the one closest to the open door. Making as much noise as possible, I open the lid and dump my "garbage" in. But no one comes out of the room.

I stand in front of the door and listen. There is no sound at all. I push the door with one finger, so that I might have just accidentally bumped it. It swings wide open.

It's a tiny little room, almost a closet, with dingy walls, a concrete floor, and one lightbulb dangling from the ceiling in a way that's slightly creepy. There's a tiny painted-over window high up on the back wall that lets in some light from outside. But not much.

The only thing in the room is a folding table with spindly metal legs. Sitting cross-legged on the table is a girl with short dark hair and bangs that draw a straight line across her forehead. She looks about seven years old.

"You came!" she says. She's wearing fuzzy pink slippers. There's an open book in her lap.

"Uh, no. I was actually just throwing out some garbage," I say. "Look, I'm sorry. My dad thinks he's funny, and he was the one who—"

"Don't worry," she interrupts, "it's not *my* stupid club."

"It isn't?"

"No. I'm just here to get paid."

"Paid for what?"

"I'm a scout."

"What's that?"

"Oh, you know." She closes the book and dangles her legs off the front of the table. I can now see that her fuzzy pink slippers have little ears. And eyes. I think they might be pigs. "Scouts look for traps, setups, that kind of thing."

"How old are you?" I say. "And what kind of traps?"

"Older than I look. And who knows what kind of traps? I told you, I'm doing this for the money. I make fifty cents every thirty minutes. That's a dollar an hour. Do you think I'd be doing this for free? For a dollar I can get a pack of Chicks, Ducks, and Bunnies SweeTarts. They only sell them in April and May. That's what I'm doing later. My mom is taking me to the Chock-Nut."

I realize she means Bennie's, where I've gone almost every day of my life after school to buy a snack. Bennie has a faded blue awning that says CHOCK-NUT, but nobody actually calls it that. When I was in kindergarten and first grade, Bennie would slide a plastic milk crate under the counter for me to stand on so I could see the candy better. I wonder if he does the same for this girl. I think how Bennie is a good guy.

She hops down from the table, landing silently in her pig slippers. "But once I get there, I might go for a Cadbury Crème Egg instead—that's another seasonal candy."

"But—who's paying you?" I ask.

"Safer is paying me."

"What's *Safer?*"

"Safer is not a what. He's the twelve-year-old human standing right behind you."

I whirl around and find myself standing nose to nose with the dog boy.

"I'm Safer," the dog boy says.

"One dollar, please!" The girl holds out her palm.

Safer takes a folded dollar bill out of his back pocket and hands it to her.

"Wait," I say. "You were sitting there for an *hour?*"

"Fifteen minutes," she says. "Plus forty-five more on the lobbycam during lunch."

"The lobbycam?"

"Yup. Watching you and your dad go out for pizza. It took you exactly forty-three minutes, in case you're wondering."

Before I can ask her what the heck she's talking about, Safer pushes her out the door. "*Goodbye,* Candy," he says to the back of her head. "Tell Mom I'll be up in a little bit."

"Wait," I say when he's closed the door behind her. "Her name is Candy?"

Safer looks at me. "Yeah."

"And your name is—Safer?"

"Yeah."

I smile. I have a strong feeling that I've just met two kids who will never make fun of my name.

Safer

"Coffee?" Safer asks.

He takes a flask—an actual *flask*—out of his back pocket. I know what a flask is because Dad has two of them. Dad doesn't use his, though. He just likes to look at them. They're really old (of course), and one of them belonged to his grandfather. It even has his initials on it.

Safer unscrews the top slowly, puts the flask to his lips, and tips it back. He swallows and then holds it out to me.

"No thanks," I say. "I heard coffee stunts your growth."

Safer shrugs, screws the top back on, and shoves the flask back into his pocket.

"Let's get started. Question number one: How many garbage cans are lined up outside that door?"

We're kind of leaning against the table from opposite sides, and he's looking right into my eyes.

"Was that your sister?" I ask.

Safer blinks. "Yes. How many garbage cans?"

"I don't know," I tell him. "Do you want me to count

them for you? Or you could, you know, count them yourself. Are you asking me to count them?"

"No. I'm not asking you to count them. I assume you can count. I'm asking you to remember."

"Oh." I realize it's a test. "Eight, maybe?"

"Ten. How many buttons on your shirt? Don't look."

I have an almost-irresistible urge to look down. I stare at the lightbulb on the ceiling to stop myself.

"Seven?"

"Eight."

"Okay. So—what's your point?"

"My point?" He pulls the flask out again, takes a drink, and wipes his mouth with his sleeve. "My point is that we have a lot of work to do."

Safer takes the spy stuff very seriously. He tells me that there's this guy in the building, who he calls Mr. X, who is almost definitely up to something evil. He says that—*evil*—like it's something he deals with every day. Just another day, fighting the world's evil forces. I like it.

Mr. X wears black all the time, Safer tells me: "All. The. Time." Black pants, black shirt, black shorts in the summer. He's always moving these suitcases in and out of the building. And they look heavy.

"Wait," I say, thinking of that morning in the elevator, "does he wear a baseball cap with a fish on it?"

Safer snaps his head around to stare at me. "No. He does not wear a baseball cap with a fish on it."

"Oh. I thought maybe I saw him. My dad talked to a guy

with two big suitcases in the elevator this morning. But he was wearing a fish hat. It was yellow."

Safer looks annoyed. "That couldn't have been him. If Mr. X wore a baseball cap, it would be black."

"Oh, right."

"And another thing is that Mr. X doesn't talk."

"He doesn't talk?"

"He doesn't talk."

"Wait—you mean, *never?*"

Safer leans toward me and shakes his head slowly back and forth. He's giving me the willies, and I'm not sure I want to be here anymore. But I'm not sure I want to leave, either.

Safer begins to pace. The room is so small that he's basically just walking around the table in a circle. Every time he gets to where I'm standing, he does an about-face and walks in the other direction.

"If we're going to work together, you have to learn to focus—try to notice things."

"What things?"

"It doesn't matter what things. Anything. Buttons. Garbage cans. Stay in the moment. I get the feeling your mind wanders."

I don't say anything. It does.

"You're a very important part of this case, you know."

"I am?"

"You are."

"Why?"

"Because you live in the apartment right below him."

"Below who?"

"Below Mr. X."

"I do? But I haven't even told you what apartment I live in."

He crosses his arms and looks at me. "I can tell you're smart, you know. Even though you ask all those questions you know the answers to."

Sure, I'm smart. And sometimes I do ask questions I know the answers to—Mom calls it stalling. But honestly, it's just hard to follow Safer's conversation.

"No one can know about this, of course. Not yet."

"About what?"

"Mr. X. Us. The Spy Club."

"Oh. What about Candy?"

"Candy won't tell. You didn't say anything, did you? To your dad?"

"No—well, he knows about the Spy Club sign—he was actually the one who asked what time the meeting was."

Safer blows out his cheeks in exasperation and throws his arms toward the ceiling. "Great! Now he knows something is up!"

"You're the one who put the sign up! What was I supposed to do? Spend twenty minutes throwing out the garbage? He'd come down here looking for me."

"It's okay," Safer says. "Calm down."

"I'm calm." I don't point out that he's the one who started throwing his arms around.

"Just tell him that no one showed."

"What?"

"Tell him you came down and waited, but no one showed up. You can do that, can't you?"

"I guess, but—"

"Good."

"Can I ask you a question? Why did you take those dogs down here? This is where those stairs lead, from the lobby, right? To the basement?"

"It's a job. I'm a dog walker."

"You walk them in the basement?"

"In the courtyard—there's a door."

"Why don't you take them outside?"

He waves a hand at me. "I had some trouble. I'm not supposed to talk about it."

"Oh." I nod toward the elevator. "So, you heading upstairs?"

"Go ahead," Safer says. "I never use the elevator. Too easy to be taken by surprise."

"Seriously?"

"And there's only one exit."

"Okay, well, I'll see you, I guess."

He nods. "At the next meeting."

"When's that?"

Safer cups one hand under my elbow and steers me to the door. "I'll be in touch."

"Should I give you my phone number or something?"

He taps his head. "Not necessary."

Fortunes

Dad is all smiles when I open the apartment door. "How'd it go?"

"No one showed," I say.

The smile drops off his face. "Oh. I'm sorry, bud."

"I don't mind," I tell him.

"You were waiting all this time?"

"Yeah—it was fine, though."

"You sure you aren't disappointed?"

Why do parents ask questions like that?

"Seriously, Dad. I'm one hundred percent *fine*."

Except that I have just lied. I hate lying. And I don't even know why I did it.

Dad says, "How about we go to Yum Li's for dinner tonight?"

Yum Li's is one of my favorite restaurants of all time. I feel kind of guilty because I know he's suggesting it to cheer me up about something that didn't really happen, but I say, "Yeah, Yum Li's sounds good," and let Dad squeeze my shoulder and pat me on the head.

"Why don't you get started on your room," he says. "I'll finish up these bookshelves."

When I think of all the work Dad put into our house it's pretty sad. But mostly I feel sorry for myself, because the coolest thing about it was my room. A long time ago, Dad took apart a fire escape—a real fire escape, from a building that his office was demolishing—and he rebuilt the bottom level of it inside my bedroom. He bolted it to the wall, and even attached the original ladder. I had a bed up there, and he made me these built-in cubbies for all my stuff. I had the most excellent room of any kid I know, and we had to leave it behind.

"It's built in," Dad explained. "Part of the house. And the buyers love it."

So do I, I wanted to tell him. But I didn't, because he looked so miserable.

At our new place, I have Dad's old bedroom furniture from when he was a kid—a bed, a desk, and a bookshelf, all made out of the same dark wood. His mom kept it in her garage all these years, and a couple of weeks ago Dad drove it to Brooklyn in a rented van.

I start to unpack my boxes, wondering whether there's a kid in my room at this very moment, climbing up and down my ladder and putting his stuff in my cubbies.

We're crossing the lobby on our way to Yum Li's when I see Candy and a woman who must be her mom coming in through the front door. Candy's lips are stained bright blue.

"Hello," the woman says, smiling and holding the door for us. Dad says hi back and I wave at Candy, but she stares straight ahead as if she doesn't even see me. I forgot that we're not supposed to know each other.

"They must live in the building," Dad says when we're outside. "I wonder if that little girl has any older brothers or sisters."

"She does." Oops.

"She does? When did you—"

"I mean, *probably* she does. She looks like the little-sister type." Now I'm feeling guilty again.

He gives me a funny look, and so I do what Candy did—just stare straight ahead and act as if I don't notice.

At Yum Li's, I forget all about feeling guilty. Just looking at the food on other people's tables makes my mouth water. We order soup, scallion pancakes, cold noodles with sesame sauce, and spicy shredded beef with broccoli.

Yum Li's isn't like most Chinese restaurants, where they rush the food out right away. Here, you have to wait. No bowls of crunchy noodles and orange goop, either. It's just ice water and the smell of other people's dinners.

Once Mom told Yum Li that he could have a big classy restaurant in Manhattan if he wanted to. "The big-business types would pay triple for your food," she told him.

But Yum Li looked around at his peeling wood paneling, laminated menus, and hanging plants, and said, "What, more classy than this?"

I shake some vinegar into my hot and sour soup and stir it in. Dad only likes won ton soup, even though sometimes

Yum Li teases him: "That's kid soup!" he tells Dad. "Time to grow up!"

Dad wants to talk. I can tell by the way he leans toward me and says "So? Tell me things!" Which is his playful way of asking me to pour my heart out.

"You tell *me* things," I say. I'm just being dumb, but he gets this serious look on his face and says, "Okay. Well, today has been tough. It's really hitting me, I guess, that—on top of, you know, everything—the house is someone else's now." He fishes in his soup for the last won ton dumpling. "I had a good talk with Mom on the phone," he says. "She sounds really— good. And it's been great to have your help today."

I don't want to think about Dad needing me. I wish I had just told him something about school instead of asking him to tell me stuff instead. I could have told him about volleyball, maybe. About the slow clap, and Dallas's foot in my stomach. But it's too late now because it feels like all that would only make him feel worse.

Dad leans back to give the waitress room to put down the rest of our food. "You remember how to get home from school tomorrow, right? To the new place?"

"Dad, are you serious? The apartment is closer to school than our house was. Is. Whatever." The point is that we're still living in the same square mile of Brooklyn where I've spent my whole life.

We stop talking and eat everything, and I mean everything, including the cut-up oranges that come with the check.

"You were hungry," the waitress says, studying the orange peels. Dad has scraped out the bitter white stuff with his teeth—according to him, it's full of vitamins. She puts a little plate on the table: our fortune cookies.

Fortunes are another thing about Yum Li's. They're not normal.

Dad cracks his cookie open, pulls an extra-long fortune out of it, and reads aloud: *"I read an article about those dark splotches on the sidewalk, and it turns out"*—he flips the fortune over to read from the back—*"those splotches are all chewed-up, spit-out, walked-on gum. Next time use the garbage can!"*

He looks up at me. "I don't even chew gum!"

I open my cookie. My fortune says, *Why don't you look up once in a while? Is something wrong with your neck?*

Like I said: not normal.

When we leave the restaurant, Dad and I start walking home in the wrong direction, and we don't even realize it until we're in front of Sixth Sense Driving School on the corner. Neither of us points out that we were walking toward our house. We just turn around.

At the apartment, I stretch out on the bed and think about how Dad used to lie right here when he was a kid. He probably never thought about the fact that his own son would be lying in his bed one day. I wonder whether Dad and I would have been friends, or if he would have been friends with Dallas Llewellyn, or Carter Dixon, or what. It's kind of a bummer to think your own dad might have been someone who called you Gorgeous.

Dad comes in, looking around the room. He's always looking. He nods approvingly at the bookshelf, where I've stuffed all my books and games. The Scrabble box got stepped on at some point, and the letter tiles went everywhere. I rescued most of them and piled them on the desk. Dad plops into the desk chair and starts making neat little stacks out of them. He can't help himself.

"So," he says. "What do you think so far?"

"It's good," I tell him.

He reaches out to pat the bed and then shifts over to sit on the edge of the mattress. "I forgot to buy breakfast stuff. Want to wake up early and eat at the diner before school?"

"Sure."

"Great."

We say goodnight. From the bed, I can see into the hall and a little into Mom and Dad's room. He's got some music on low, and he's putting their bed together with a wrench. The phone rings, and I hear Dad say, "Hey, Lisa." Mom's older sister.

"Yeah," he says, "everything is stable." Then his voice drops.

It's weird that the ceiling is so far away. At home on my fire escape, I could almost reach up and touch it. I feel smaller.

I'm trying to get comfortable when I feel something under my pillow. I pull it out—an index card. Tilting it to catch the light from the hall, I read:

NEXT MEETING TOMORROW
—S.

I bolt upright, flick on the light, and look around. Safer has been here. In my room.

I walk around, opening the closet door and squinting

through the window to the fire escape. I get back into bed, and then I jump up again to look underneath it. But there's no sign of anyone.

This is when I realize that Safer might be what Mom calls an unknown quantity. In other words, even weirder than I thought.

Salty

I'm stuffing schoolbooks into my backpack the next morning when I see that Dad's Scrabble-tile towers have been razed.

Spelled out across the desk are three words:

LOVE YOU PICKLE

For one crazy second I think of Safer, that maybe he somehow got in here again when I was asleep, and I'm still staring at the words when Dad sticks his head in.

"Message from Mom," he says quietly. He tries to catch my eyes but I don't let him.

Right. Safer does not love me, and he does not call me Pickle.

Mom's job is officially the day shift, seven a.m. to three p.m. It takes her half an hour to report to the next charge nurse on duty and forty-five minutes to drive home. If a nurse on the next shift calls in sick, Mom can be "held over" to work the first half of the three-to-eleven shift, and someone else gets called in to cover the second half. That's called a split.

But if they can't find anyone to come in for the second half of the split, Mom has to work the whole three-to-eleven shift, which means she works from seven a.m. to eleven p.m. That's called a double.

We all hated doubles until Dad lost his job. Then Mom started volunteering for them whenever she could. I still hate them, though.

Dad's in the doorway again. He's wearing a tie, and his "client meeting" glasses, with the rectangular black frames. "Almost ready?" he asks in a low voice. We're always quiet before school, because when Mom works doubles, the number-one rule of the morning is not to wake her up.

"One sec," I say. And, rearranging the Scrabble letters with two fingers, I quickly spell:

HAVE A GOOD DAY
LOVE ME

First period. Science. The science lab is different from the other classrooms—it has these old thick wood tables with black marks burned into them, and metal stools to sit on. It's the only room at school that makes me think of all the kids who were here before us. I look at the scratches and the burn marks, and I think about how each one happened on a particular day, maybe twenty or forty years ago, and how each mark was made by a particular person. Those people are probably scattered all over the country now. Some of them could be dead.

Dallas Llewellyn passes me on the way to his seat, saying "You're it, Gorgeous," and flicking the top of my ear with his finger. I ignore him. Dallas is always on the lookout for other people's weak spots so that he knows exactly where to poke them. And if you don't have a weak spot, he'll invent one and poke you anyway.

Mr. Landau writes TASTE on the whiteboard.

"Taste-*test*, Taste-*test*," Carter Dixon chants. He's pounding his fists on Table Two. Mandy giggles and gives him a thumbs-up. Everyone knows that she hopes the taste test will reveal that she and Gabe are destined to fall in love and be together forever.

Mr. Landau doesn't hear Carter, or doesn't want to. But sometime next week, he'll hand out these little strips of paper, and when he tells us to, we'll all put them in our mouths. The paper is coated with some kind of horrible-tasting chemical, so everyone will go running for the water fountain. Almost everyone. Some people can't taste the chemical at all, and to them the paper will just taste like paper. Those couple of kids will be left sitting on their stools and wondering why everyone else looks like they're going to puke.

And they'll be looking around to see who else is sitting there with them.

Here's the story:

A long time ago, the only two kids who didn't run for water were a boy and a girl who started dating when they got to high school. People say they got married, but I've never seen any proof. Another year, there was only one kid in the whole class who didn't taste the chemical stuff, and he got killed by a drunk driver the summer after his sophomore year. So someone decided that the taste test is the universe's way of revealing fate: love or death. And of course everyone else fell for it right away.

Today Mr. Landau is talking about salty. He's passed around these stale mini-pretzels, and we're eating them. We're supposed to chew slowly and take notes about what we taste, without using the word *salty*. I write down *zingy*. I think about writing *stale* or *crummy*, but I don't want to hurt anyone's feelings.

I'm not much in the mood for stale pretzels because I just had the double-stack pancake special at Everybody's Favorite Diner. It's not actually everybody's favorite, but that's what the restaurant is called: Everybody's Favorite Diner. Dad says the owner is a genius.

Mr. Landau asks us to "share our observations." When no one does, he starts calling on people.

"It's salty," Dallas Llewellyn says, shrugging.

Mr. Landau sighs. Then he takes this red and white plastic cooler out of the supply closet, puts it on his desk, and opens it. We can see a big plastic jug with ice packed around it.

He asks Gabe to hand out some tiny paper cups, and then he walks around the classroom with the plastic jug, filling each cup with a tiny amount of mystery liquid.

"Don't drink it," he says. "Just taste. Let it sit on your tongue." He pours a bit into his own cup, leans back against his desk, and tips the cup into his mouth.

We do the same.

The liquid is salty and cold.

"It's just salty water," someone says.

Mr. Landau nods. "But salty *how*? How is this sensation of salt different from the pretzel?"

Gabe says, "That was dry salty. This is wet salty."

But it's more than that. This taste reminds me of dirt, or animals, or skin. I swish around what's left in my cup, thinking.

"Is it—is it *tears*?" one of the girls says.

"Ew!"

It isn't tears. I know what it is. I decide to drink my cupful, tipping my head back.

"Gross!" Dallas yells, "Georges drank a whole thing of tears!"

Everyone starts screeching.

"Relax!" Mr. Landau calls out. "It's not a big deal. It's not tears." He looks at me: "But I did say not to drink it."

Dallas tries for another minute to make it seem completely catastrophic that I drank an ounce of salt water. But the moment has passed.

"Georges," Mr. Landau says as we're filing out the door to math, "do you have a second?"

"You doing okay?" he asks me when we're alone.

"I'm good," I tell him.

"If you ever want to talk, I'm here."

Sensitive-moment alert. "I knew it wasn't tears," I say. "That's just—stupid."

"Right," he says. "Where would a person get that many tears?"

Which makes me wonder: If you took every tear cried by everyone on earth on one single day and put them in a container, how big would that container need to be? Could you fill a water tower? Three water towers? It's one of those unknowable things. There has to be an answer, but we'll never know what it is.

I tap the red and white cooler. "It wasn't just salt water, though, right? It was ocean water."

He smiles. "Correct."

I get this picture in my head of Mr. Landau with his cooler and his plastic bottles, heading out to Coney Island on the Q train.

"I figured it wouldn't matter if I drank it. When I swim at Cape Cod, I always drink a bunch of water by accident."

He nods.

"And even if it was tears—who cares? I mean, why are people so afraid of everything?"

"Georges?"

"Yes?"

"Are you trying to engage me in a philosophical discussion so that you can miss part of math?"

I smile. My mouth feels stretched out, like it might be my first smile of the day. "Maybe."

"Go to math."

"Okay." I walk away, quizzing myself: twenty-eight stools in the room, ten buttons on Mr. Landau's shirt, four pencils and two pens in the cup on his desk.

Uncle

On the way home from school, I stop at Bennie's to buy a pack of Starbursts. I notice a pile of Chicks, Ducks, and Bunnies SweeTarts and think again how weird it is that Candy's name is Candy. Not that I'm judging.

Bennie is chatting, which means I have to wait to pay, because Bennie does only one thing at a time. I debate the morality of eating a Starburst before the pack is paid for and decide not to.

"Do you know a girl named Candy?" I ask Bennie when he comes to the register.

"Sure do," he says. "One of my best customers."

I give him my dollar and he counts out my change: "Seventy-five cents for the Starbursts!" he announces. "A nickel makes *eighty*, a dime makes *ninety*, and another dime is *one dollar*." That's another thing about Bennie—he always counts your change back to you.

"Do you know her brother—Safer?"

"The tall guy?"

"No—like my size."

Bennie shakes his head. "Don't know him."

"Did you know that she calls this place the Chock-Nut? Candy does, I mean."

I didn't even know I was going to say that. It all just seems so weird, how I thought Bennie's was kind of my place all these years and it turns out to be some other person's place, too—and some other person might even be one of Bennie's best customers, but she calls it the Chock-Nut.

He shrugs. "That's what it says on the sign."

"But what do *you* call it?"

"Me?" He cracks open a roll of dimes against the edge of the counter. "I call it work."

I'm in the lobby of our building, waiting for the elevator, when a teenage girl walks in with a boy who's maybe four years old. The girl is talking on her cell phone, saying, "I'm telling you, forget it. Vanessa holds a grudge forever. *Forever!*"

We all stand and look at the arrow that shows what floor the elevator's on.

"Six! Five! Four!" the little kid yells, and then he starts spinning in circles, just for fun. I remember doing that.

The elevator comes, and we get on, the boy bumping into the walls because he's dizzy from the spinning. He leans back into a corner and looks up at me, all woozy.

"Knock, knock," he says.

"Who's there?" I say.

"Interrupting cow."

"Interrupting cow wh—"

"MOOOOO! MOOOOOO!"

The kid totally cracks up. He's laughing so hard he almost falls over. Unless he's just still really dizzy. They get off on two, with the girl still on the phone. I can hear the kid laughing even after the elevator door closes behind them.

My stupid key sticks in the lock, and it takes me three tries to get the apartment door open. The whole time I'm fiddling with it, I can hear the phone ringing inside.

"Hello?"

"MOOOO!"

It's actually even weirder than you might be thinking. I sort of shake my head and try again.

"Hello?"

"It's Safer."

"Oh. Hi. How did you know about the—?"

"Apartment 6A. Come on up."

I'm supposed to call Mom or Dad after school so they know I got home okay. Dad has a meeting with a "potential big client," which he says is good news for our "potential summer vacation at the Cape," where we always rent a house for two weeks, except last summer, when we didn't.

I call him on his cell, and then I quick call Mom because Dad says I have to. Her number at the hospital is stuck to the refrigerator with a magnet. She sounds tired. I tell her school was good, lunch was good, coming home was good, I don't have a lot of homework, and yes, I will make myself a snack. I don't tell her about Carter Dixon's incredibly stupid new "gay test," which has something to do with what finger is longer than some other finger.

I run up the three flights to 6A. I ring the bell. A thumping sound comes closer and closer, and then the door flings open. It's Candy. There's a long hallway stretching behind her.

"Grand tour!" she announces, pumping one fist into the air. She pivots and marches away from me, leading me down the hall with her hand up in the air as if I might otherwise lose her.

She points as we pass a series of doors. "My room, Safer's room, bathroom, Pigeon's room, bathroom, Mom and Dad's room, Mom's photography studio—quiet, she's in there working—kitchen, dining room, and here's the living room."

It's a big apartment. I wonder if Safer and Candy go to private school.

In one corner of the living room, I see Safer, sunk into a beanbag chair, reading. He doesn't look up. I can see only the top of his head and his legs from the knees down.

"Safer!" Candy shouts at him. "Your friend is here!"

She turns to me. "You have to talk loud when he's reading. Otherwise he just ignores you." Then she marches away, down the hallway.

"Welcome to Uncle," Safer says.

"Uh, thanks."

"You know what *Uncle* means, right? It's spy slang for the headquarters of an espionage organization."

"Oh. But I thought your office was in the basement."

He makes a face. "It's nicer up here, don't you think?"

I look around at the couches, the rugs, and the beanbag chairs. "It's definitely nicer up here," I say.

"So. Have you been practicing?"

"Yeah. At school, a little."

"What was Candy wearing? Start with the feet."

"Um, shoes?"

"Bare feet," he says. "What else?"

"Jeans?"

"Carpenter pants."

"What are carpenter pants?"

"Let's switch subjects. I'm going to train you on the lobbycam."

He walks over to the intercom, which is attached to the wall near the kitchen. It matches the one in our apartment: a white plastic square with what looks like a tiny little television screen set into it, and three buttons underneath, labeled VIEW, TALK, and DOOR.

"I already know how to use it," I say. "My dad showed me. You push View to get the picture on the screen. You push Talk to talk to whoever is down in the lobby. You push Door to buzz them in."

"You know how to use it as an intercom. But do you know how to use it as an observation tool?"

He pushes the View button. The screen flickers, and then the lobby comes into focus. "What do you see?"

"The door in the lobby."

"What else?"

"Nothing. The floor."

"Very good." He nods and continues to gaze at the screen. "Now what?" I say.

He takes a spiral notebook from his back pocket, flips it open, and pulls a pen from behind his ear. "Now we wait."

"Just standing here, you mean?"

"Of course not. We can bring stools from the kitchen."

"Ewwww! There's stool in the kitchen? Gross!" Candy runs into the hallway from her bedroom. I make a mental note that she is now wearing a sundress and her fuzzy pig slippers.

She stops in front of me. "Do you know what *stool* means? What it *really* means?"

"Cut it out, Candy!" Safer tells her.

"*Stool* means 'poop,'" Candy tells me. "It's the *real* word for it, the one that doctors use."

"CANDY!" a woman's voice says from somewhere. "Enough!"

Candy rolls her eyes and disappears into her room.

"Is that true?" I ask Safer while we carry two wooden stools from the kitchen.

"Yeah," he says, "it is, actually." We push the stools together in front of the little intercom screen. Safer goes back into the kitchen and reappears thirty seconds later with his flask.

"Coffee?" he asks, holding it out.

I tell him no thanks. We watch the lobby door.

We watch the lobby door some more.

Then we watch the lobby door a little more.

"Does this ever get boring?" I ask.

He looks like he can't believe me. "No," he says. "It doesn't get boring. Boredom is what happens to people who have no control over their minds."

"Oh."

I tell myself that no matter what, I will not speak for the

next ten minutes. I will not take my eyes off the lobbycam. I will not even look at my watch.

We stare at the screen. Every once in a while it goes dark because there's an automatic timer that shuts it off, and Safer has to push the button to make the picture come back. When I am positively, absolutely, one hundred percent sure ten minutes have passed, I check my watch.

Six minutes.

Safer is completely intent upon the screen, his pen hovering over his spiral notebook.

At first I try to stifle my yawns, but it's hopeless. I'm yawning and yawning. Safer doesn't catch a single yawn. Maybe the coffee helps.

I think I'm falling asleep when Safer says "Look!" He elbows me in the ribs and I almost fall off my stool, knocking his pen on the floor. I bend over to pick it up and smack my head against the wall. I stand up with one hand on my forehead.

"You missed it!" Safer says. He snatches his pen from my hand and scribbles in his notebook. He grabs my wrist, looks at my watch and mumbles, "Four-fifty-one."

"What?" I say. "What happened? Four-fifty-one *what*?"

"It was him. Mr. X."

"No way."

"Way."

"What was he doing?"

"Coming into the building. With his key."

"Oh. Right. What was he wearing? Was he wearing black? Did he have any suitcases?"

"Of course he was wearing black. I told you, he *only* wears black. No suitcases this time. But he looked . . ."

I wait. "He looked like what?"

Safer clicks his pen a few times. "He looked furtive."

"Furtive," I repeat.

"It means 'secretive.'"

"I know what it means."

"Don't feel bad," Safer says. "You're still in training, remember?"

I think about what Candy said, that it took me and Dad forty-three minutes to get pizza. A tiny little kid can sit still in front of this thing without falling asleep, but I can't.

Something occurs to me: "How did Candy know we went for pizza yesterday?" I ask Safer. "We didn't bring it home. We ate at DeMarco's."

He looks at me thoughtfully. "Good question. Let's ask her."

"Oh, that's okay, I don't need to—"

"Candy!"

In two seconds, Candy is in front of us. In case Safer decides to quiz me, I take note that she's changed again, into overalls (denim, with front and back pockets) and a long-sleeved green T-shirt. She's still wearing the pig slippers.

"How did you know that Georges and his dad went for pizza yesterday?" Safer asks her.

"Cup," she answers.

He nods.

"What?" I say.

"It was a cup," Safer says. "Were you or your dad carrying one?"

Then I remember that Dad had a lemonade from the fountain at DeMarco's, and he finished it on the way home. The cup must have been in his hand when we came in.

"You memorized what the cups look like at DeMarco's?"

She shrugs. "Everyone goes to DeMarco's. I've been going there my whole life."

"Well, so have I," I tell her.

"Then close your eyes," Safer says. "Don't you know what their cups look like?"

I close my eyes. "White," I say, "and there's writing . . . *Have a Nice Day* or something like that. . . ."

"Thank You for Coming," Candy says.

"Yeah—*Thank You for Coming*! Written over and over, in a spiral. And the letters are green and red?"

Candy claps for me and then heads back to her room. To change clothes again, I'm guessing.

Safer nods at me. "Now you're beginning to think like one of us."

I guess I am.

I have to go downstairs to start homework. Safer walks me down the hallway toward his front door.

"Safer?"

"Yeah?"

"Who's Pigeon?"

"My brother."

"Is he here?"

"No. He's never here. See you at the next meeting."

"When's that?"

"I'll be in touch."

Which reminds me. "Safer?"

"Yes?"

"How did you get into my room yesterday?"

"Oh, I come and go," he says.

I don't say anything.

"Wait—did it bother you?"

"Kind of."

"Say no more. It won't happen again."

I smile. "Thanks."

Downstairs, I can't find my protractor, which I need for geometry. I go into Dad's bedroom closet, where he crammed all the drawing supplies that used to be in his home office, behind our old kitchen. As soon as I pull the light cord, I see a stack of Mom's nursing uniforms on a shelf, perfectly folded into neat Dad-squares, with one of her plastic name-tag pins resting on top. I decide to forget about homework. I chill out with Sir Ott on the couch and watch some *America's Funniest Home Videos* instead. When Dad gets home, he looks worn out. We order from the bad pizza place with the yellowy cheese. I tell him I met a kid in the building, because I know it will make his day, and it does.

The phone rings a few times, and Dad goes into his room to talk with the door closed. Maybe it's another potential client.

I leave Mom a note with the Scrabble tiles:

WISH DEMARCOS DELIVERED

LOVE ME

Bittersweet

Mom's morning Scrabble note says:

BEATS HOSPITAL FOOD

The only good thing about when Mom works a double is that, along with the extra pay, she gets a two-hour card. A two-hour card is worth two hours of work—mostly she uses it to sleep in and start her morning shift two hours late, but sometimes she uses a two-hour card to leave work early and surprise me after school. She'll be waiting right by the front doors, smiling away, and we'll head over to Bennie's before walking home. Bennie always makes a big deal out of Mom, pretending he's in love with her. She reminds him of someone back in Egypt, he says, but he never tells who.

First period. Science.
We file in, Dallas and Carter walking close behind me.

"Beep, beep, beep, beep," Dallas says. "Beep-beep-beep-beep."

"What's that noise?" Carter asks. "Dallas, is your freak alarm going off?"

"Yeah, it's going crazy. I wonder why. Oh, look, it's just Georges."

They shove past me, laughing.

Mr. Landau writes on the board:

> **Sweet**
> **Salty**
> **Sour**
> **Bitter**

Then he turns around to face us. "There's one more," he says. "Does anyone know what it is?"

No one does.

Underneath *Bitter*, he writes:

> **Umami**

"You *mama*," Gabe says.

Everyone cracks up. Especially Mandy.

Mr. Landau looks at Gabe. "You know, someone makes that same comment almost every single year." He sighs, like he's really bored. "I just never know who it'll be."

The class laughs even harder. Score one for Mr. Landau. He could teach Ms. Warner a thing or two. I wonder if they ever go out for coffee or anything.

"Umami," Mr. Landau says, "is often referred to as the fifth taste. Has anyone ever heard of it?"

No one has.

"Umami is a savory taste. Think of excellent Chinese food, a steak, or a perfectly ripe tomato."

At which point Mandy has to tell everyone for the hundredth time that ever since she saw her little brother throw up at DeMarco's last summer, she can't even think about eating anything with tomatoes.

"I'm very sorry to hear that," Mr. Landau tells her. He turns back to the board and numbers the tastes, one through five:

1. Sweet
2. Salty
3. Sour
4. Bitter
5. Umami

"Everyone take out a clean piece of paper!"

We get out paper and look at him. He makes us wait a few beats, and then he says, "What is the taste of human experience?"

Oh, boy. The room is quiet.

"Can a moment in time be sweet? Can a memory be bitter? I want each of you to spend the next twenty minutes writing about a memory that can be described using the metaphor of taste. Table One, you will write about a sweet memory. Table Two, a salty memory. And so on."

Every hand at Table Five immediately shoots into the air. Mr. Landau calls on Natasha.

"An *umami* memory?" she asks.

Mr. Landau tells her to think of umami as meaning "delicious."

Natasha nods and starts writing immediately.

* * *

Table Six is just me and Bob English Who Draws. There is no sixth taste on the board. We look at each other. I know he won't raise his hand, because he never does, and he knows I won't raise mine, because I never do either. We sort of shrug at each other.

"I almost forgot," Mr. Landau says. He goes up to the whiteboard, writes the word *bittersweet*, and puts a 6 next to it. "Twenty minutes."

My bittersweet memory: Jason and I are six or seven, grocery shopping with my mom. We're outside the Met Foods on Flatbush, and it's a sunny fall day. Jason and I are looking at some big plastic balls in a wire bin on the sidewalk by the front doors. Mom is waiting for us.

We're about to go inside the store when we hear this thump, like someone has bounced a Super Ball against the store window, only there's no one there, and no ball.

Then we see the bird lying on the sidewalk. It's tiny and brown and in a bad position, and Jason begins to freak out. I want to cry because I think maybe we did something that killed the bird.

The first thing Mom does is pull us into a huddle and tell us that it isn't our fault. What happened was that the sun was shining so hard against the store window that the glass reflected the trees on the other side of the street and the bird didn't even know the window was there. The bird thought it was flying into the air and the trees, just like on any other day.

She has us breathe. Then she turns to the bird, and says, "Look."

We look. The bird is pulsing—its neck is sort of vibrating. Jason gets scared, thinking that it's having an attack or something, but Mom explains that it's just the bird's heart beating. Bird hearts beat very fast.

"The bird is alive," she tells us. "It must have been stunned when it hit the window."

And just then the bird's head snaps back to a right-looking position on its neck, and it hops up and shakes itself. We start laughing and slapping each other five.

Mom says this calls for a celebration. She lets us each choose a plastic ball out of the wire bin, and she buys them for us.

I have no idea where that ball is now, and I'm pretty sure Jason didn't keep his either.

I don't write any of this down on my paper, of course. In fact, I don't write anything down.

I glance at Bob English Who Draws and see that he isn't writing either. He's drawing a supervillain with pointy ears and a billowing black cape. He must feel me watching, because he looks over, then jots something down and shoves his notebook over to me.

On one corner of the page, he's written:

So dum!

I lean over and say, "You do know *dumb* has a *b* on the end of it, right?"

"Haven't you heard of spelling reform?" he asks in a low voice.

"No."

"I spell it like it sounds. Benjamin Franklin and Teddy Roosevelt both believed in it," he says. "Look it up."

"Okay."

"Ask yourself: Does that *b* serve a purpose? Why is it even there?"

"Mr. English!" Mr. Landau snaps. "Shall I presume that you have finished your work and are ready to share it with the class?"

Bob English hunches over his drawing and says nothing. I don't say anything either. But what I'm thinking is that *dum* just looks—kind of dumb.

chicken is chickens

Lunch. The hot lunch is pasta with meat sauce. It's actually delicious. Maybe not *umami* delicious, but pretty darn tasty. Hardly any of the other kids will eat it, because if you eat anything other than a dry, crumbly bagel for lunch at this school you are basically announcing yourself as a freak. You might as well be walking around without pants.

But I eat the hot lunch. I figure that life will have its share of dry bread, and that when there is meat sauce on the table, I should eat it. And I do.

I'm finishing my garlic knot when Jason walks over to me with his tray. He is not coming to sit. He is on his way from the cool table to the garbage cans. I am a point on that line.

"Hey," he says.

"Hey."

"My mom says you guys sold your house."

I nod. "Yeah."

"You moved into an apartment?"

"Yeah."

"Did you bring the fire escape?"

"No. We had to leave it."

"Oh. Dude—sorry. About that."

I raise my shoulders and drop them. "Stuff happens."

"Yeah. Your parents are still cool, though, right? So I bet it'll be, you know, okay."

"You're right," I tell Jason. "It will be okay. It already is."

He nods and walks away.

It's hard to hate him, even though he kind of shrugged off our friendship like it was nothing, because I've been watching him all year, and underneath that skateboarder outfit, he's the same person he always was. I don't know whether that makes it harder or easier. I watch Jason tip his tray into the garbage. His bagel wrapper sticks, and he takes the time to peel it off before he adds his tray to the stack.

After school, Bennie counts back my change and tells me, "I saw your friend today."

"Who?"

"Candy."

"Oh," I say, stuffing coins into my pocket. "She's not my friend. She lives in my new building."

"One of my best customers!" Bennie calls after me.

My key is somehow getting worse. To get the door open, I have to jiggle it in the lock and simultaneously pull the knob toward me as hard as I can. And the whole time I'm struggling, I can hear the phone ringing on the other side of the door.

"Hello?"

"Come up," Safer says.

*   *   *

Candy lets me in, and I follow her down the hallway, trying to memorize everything she's wearing for when Safer quizzes me.

She points at the living room, says, "He's in there," and then takes a left through the swinging door that leads to the kitchen. I hear her mom's voice behind the door, and then Candy's high one answering "Just Georges." I notice there's a pretty good smell in the apartment.

Safer is on his knees with a pair of binoculars raised to his eyes, looking through one of the four big windows.

"Overalls," I tell him. "Purple T-shirt, blue socks."

"Sit." He points an elbow at a green beanbag chair.

"Three hair-clip thingies," I say, plunking into the beanbag. "And some of those rubber-band bracelets."

"Okay, great. You can stop now."

"Who are you spying on?" I ask him. "Someone across the street?"

He lowers the binoculars and stares at me. "You're joking, right? If I were spying, I wouldn't want to be seen, would I? And so pressing up against the window like this would be a pretty dumb idea, wouldn't it?"

"I guess so."

"I'm watching the birds."

"What birds?"

He puts the binoculars on the windowsill, picks up his spiral notebook, and writes in it. When he's done, he flips the notebook closed and looks at me. "You know about the parrots, right?"

"What parrots?"

"The wild parrots. Nesting over there." He points to a building across the street. "See that air conditioner? With all the twigs stuffed underneath it? That's the nest."

I squint at it. "They're, like, real parrots? Where did they come from?"

"Runaway pets, maybe. Or some people think they escaped from a crate at Kennedy Airport in the 1960s."

"Wow. I didn't know parrots lived that long."

"*These* birds didn't escape—their grandparents or something, probably. They've been living over there for years. Pigeon used to watch them. He had this book where he wrote down all this stuff about them, like when they laid their eggs and when the babies hatched." He looks down at his notebook. "I'm taking notes now, in case he wants them later. My mom says he went teen-crazy but it won't last forever."

"That's nice of you."

"No it isn't. It's probably just stupid."

Candy appears in the doorway. "Mom's cooking and her hands are full of guck, but she says can Georges stay for dinner?" She looks at me. "Dad has to teach a last-minute lesson, so you might as well eat his food."

"Candy!" her mom's voice calls out. "What kind of an invitation is that?"

"Guck" doesn't actually sound all that great, but I say, "Sure, maybe, let me call my dad."

Candy smiles and retreats to the kitchen.

"Your dad's a teacher?" I ask Safer.

"Kind of. He owns a driving school."

"Is it Sixth Sense?"

"Yeah. You know it?"

"I used to walk past it every day on my way home from school."

I call Dad on his cell and ask if I can stay. He says yes, but I feel kind of bad, picturing Dad eating alone, until he tells me he's over at the hospital, saying hi to Mom, so maybe he'll just stay and have something with her.

"Want to talk to her?" he asks. "I'm down in the cafeteria, grabbing a cup of tea, but you could call back in five minutes."

I tell him Safer and I are busy right now, but that I'll get my homework done early so we can watch some baseball when he gets home. Dad sounds happy about that. The truth is that I did all my homework at school, during lunch, when other kids were talking and stuff.

When I get off the phone, Safer says, "Ready to get down to business?"

"Sure."

"We need to keep track of when Mr. X comes and goes. We're going to try out a new piece of equipment."

Phew. No lobbycam.

He holds up a gum wrapper and says, "Ta-da!"

"That's equipment?"

"The best spy equipment doesn't *look* like equipment, Georges. Here's how it works: Right before you go to bed tonight, you zip upstairs to Mr. X's and stick this gum wrapper between the door and the frame, at about knee height. When he opens the door to leave in the morning, it'll drop onto the doormat. I'll start checking really early, so I'll know when he goes out."

We're sitting in the beanbags, facing each other, so it's

hard to avoid his eyes. But I'm not sure I want to be a part of this. I mean, what if the guy opens his front door at the very moment I'm standing on his doormat fiddling with a gum wrapper?

Safer is still talking. "And then I'll put the wrapper *back* between the door and the frame, so that we'll know if he's come back. If the wrapper is still in the door when you get home from school, he hasn't come home yet. That means we have a window of opportunity."

"Opportunity for what?"

"We're not up to that part yet."

"So I have to put the gum wrapper in at night and then check it after school?"

"Exactly."

Great. So that's *twice* a day I'll be standing on the doormat of doom.

"Why a gum wrapper?"

Safer smiles. "Think about it, Georges. A piece of paper on the floor is suspicious. But a gum wrapper provides its own story—someone unwrapped a piece of gum and dropped the wrapper on the floor. People are slobs! End of story. No suspicions."

"Huh."

"Besides, we need a cover story in case one of us actually runs into Mr. X. I mean, what are we doing squatting on his doormat, right? So if you see him, all you have to do is straighten up, hold out the gum wrapper, shake your head, and say 'People are slobs!' Then walk away, nice and slow."

Safer thinks of everything. It makes it hard to turn him down.

We hang out and watch the parrots until dinner. Safer doesn't mention anything else about Mr. X, so I don't either. I learn to focus the binoculars and actually see one of the parrots fly out of the nest. Safer tells me that even though it looks like a messy bunch of sticks, the nest has three different areas, almost like little rooms.

Candy announces that dinner is ready, and then Safer's mom comes out of the kitchen. It's the first time I've actually seen her since that first night in the lobby when I had to pretend I didn't know Candy. She smiles at me and shakes my hand and tells me I'm very welcome in their home. Which is nice.

Right before we sit down to eat, the door bangs open and a thicker, much taller version of Safer walks in. He's got dark wavy hair. A pair of sneakers with the laces tied together hangs over one shoulder, and he's wearing black jeans and a faded T-shirt.

"Who's this?" he asks, pointing at me and smiling.

"Pigeon!" Safer's mom says. "Is that a hello? This is Safer's friend, Georges."

"He lives on three," Candy adds.

Pigeon's eyebrows shoot up. "Cool," he says. "Nice to meet you, Georges." He sticks out his hand, and we shake.

"Hmph." Safer slams into his chair.

"Don't mind Safer," Pigeon tells me. "He's still mad at me." He turns to Safer and puts him in a headlock. "Can't stay mad forever, buddy. I'm still the only brother you've got." Safer squirms and turns his face away. Pigeon lets him go.

The food is chicken stir-fry and rice, and it's good. Safer's mom and Pigeon pretty much carry the conversation, asking me questions about my family and school. I end up telling them about how we're studying taste in science, and about umami. I don't explain about how it's the Science Unit of Destiny, because they would all think my school is full of idiots and they don't need to know that. Safer frowns through the whole meal.

Safer's mom watches as Pigeon picks all the chicken out of his stir-fry and pushes it to one side of his plate.

She frowns. "Not with your fingers, Pigeon. And have you had any protein today?"

"Ate a bean burrito for breakfast," Pigeon says. "Ha! 'Bean burrito for breakfast.' In poetry that's called alliteration."

"*Alliteration*," Safer mimics. "Oh la *la*."

"Are you a vegetarian?" I ask Pigeon.

"No, I just don't eat birds."

"Oh."

"Tell him the story!" Candy says.

"Candy!" Safer's mom says. "Don't talk with your mouth full. Swallow, *then* talk."

Candy swallows and looks at me. "It's a really funny story."

Pigeon smiles. "Okay. So one day when I was totally little, Mom, Dad, and I are driving along this road up in Connecticut and we see these cows. And I'm like, what are cows for? I mean, what do they *do*, you know? And Mom's trying to give me the easy answer, so she tells me, 'Cows are for milk, remember? Cows give us milk.'

"But then Dad pipes up, 'And meat.' And I'm like, 'What do you mean, meat?' Then he tells me that hamburgers are

6 2

cow meat. And this lightbulb goes on in my head, and I start thinking about all the foods we eat, and I'm asking, what about dumplings, and what about bacon—and they're telling me, pork dumplings are from pigs, blah blah blah. I was real interested in all of it. It's one of those things you remember— you're just a little kid, and you're finally clueing in to the real world, you know? And so then I say, 'What about chicken? Where does chicken come from?' And right then this *other* lightbulb goes on in my head, and I start screaming, 'Chicken is *chickens?*'

"At first they thought it was funny—you know, 'Chicken is chickens,' ha ha. But I was horrified. I would rather gnaw off my own fingers than eat a bird. And that was it. No birds for me since that day in the car."

"Isn't that hilarious?" Candy says. "Chicken is chickens?"

"So what do you eat on Thanksgiving?" I ask Pigeon. Don't ask me why I'm thinking about Thanksgiving in particular. It's just the one day of the year when everyone in the country is eating a bird, I guess.

He shrugs. "Stuffing, mashed potatoes, string beans, cranberry sauce—all the side dishes. I hear turkey doesn't have a lot of flavor."

"I love turkey," Safer says. "It's delicious. I wish I could eat turkey every day."

"Safer," his mom says. "No baiting."

Safer pushes back from the table and stands up. "Come on, Georges."

"You didn't ask to be excused," Safer's mom says.

"Fine. Can Georges and I be excused?"

She smiles. "Yes. Thank you for asking."

I stand up and thank Safer's mom for dinner. She beams at me.

"Why do you hate your brother so much?" I ask Safer when we're back in the living room, sunk into the beanbag chairs.

"I don't hate him," Safer says.

"He seems nice."

"Yeah," Safer says. "He used to be nice. I wouldn't know anymore, though—he's gone all the time."

"Gone where?"

"To high school."

"School!" I laugh. "How is that his fault?"

Safer looks at me. "What do you mean, how is it his fault? It's completely his fault. He's the one who asked to go."

"Wait—don't you go to school?"

"Of course not. Neither does Candy. Neither did Pigeon, until last year."

"Seriously?"

"Ninety-five percent of school is a complete waste of time."

At which point I experience a moment when I think my friendship with Safer is somehow meant to be.

What Safer Does All Day While I'm at School

- Learns math from a website.
- Helps "prep" dinner.
- Reads.
- Plays online Scrabble with his dad between
  driving lessons.

- Walks the dogs in the courtyard.
- Has coffee with Mr. Gervais on the fifth floor. They
    read the French newspaper together, Safer says.
    Sort of.
- Watches baseball-card auctions on eBay.
- Plays chess with Candy. Candy is frighteningly good
    at chess, according to Safer.
- Learns chemistry and Photoshop from his mom.
- Watches the lobbycam.
- Watches the parrots.

When he gets home, Dad comes upstairs to meet Safer's
mom and to thank her for feeding me. He's carrying a couple
of binders and a saggy bag of groceries and looks tired, but
he gets all excited when he sees the stove in their kitchen,
which is apparently some kind of antique. Safer's mom tells
him about a warehouse right here in Brooklyn where you can
buy old appliances. Then she asks about Mom and where we
moved from and all that, and I know they're going to be a
while, so I wander into the living room.

Safer looks up from his book. "I thought you left," he says.

"Not yet."

"You want to come for breakfast tomorrow? I'll make us
eggs. I make really good scrambled eggs. I'll teach you."

"Is that a spy skill?"

He shrugs. "Spies have to eat."

"I can't. I have to leave the house by seven-forty-five. For
school."

"Oh, right."

Dad comes out of the kitchen with Safer's mom, who

gives me a long look. Then she smiles and says, "Georges, I want you to know that you are welcome here anytime. Breakfast, lunch, or dinner."

"Thanks," I say, wanting to leave all of a sudden. I look at Dad, who reads my face and says it's time to go.

Downstairs, I find the baseball game on TV while Dad puts away the stuff he bought, which turns out to be plums, chips, string cheese, and four packs of these yogurt drinks Mom likes. Then we chill out on the couch with Sir Ott, eating chips and plums and watching the game, neither of us saying that it's a lot more fun to watch baseball with Mom, who actually knows something about it. Dad asks how I'm doing, and he even turns the volume down on the television just in case I want to pour my heart out, but I don't.

Mom calls before bed and doesn't sound that tired. She asks me all about Safer's family. When I tell her Safer doesn't go to school, she says they sound like really nice bohemians. When I tell her that Safer plans to teach me the secret of truly excellent scrambled eggs, she says they sound like really smart bohemians. Dad calls them progressive. Nobody wants to say they're weird.

I give her a few play-by-plays from the Mets game, and we say goodnight.

Later, while Dad is doing his nightly murmuring-into-the-phone ritual with the door to his room closed, I slip upstairs to Mr. X's apartment and wedge Safer's balled-up gum wrapper between the door and the frame. My heart is going a mile a minute, but nothing bad happens. It's completely quiet up there.

Before bed, I spell Mom a note with the Scrabble tiles:

THE METS WON
LOVE ME

The Soft G

Mom's morning message says:

Dad is gone already, and he's left a note and bagel money on the counter. I open the refrigerator and see that two of Mom's yogurt drinks are missing.

First period. Science.

I'm sitting quietly at Table Six with Bob English Who Draws, who is drawing. Dallas pats me roughly on the head as he walks by. "Hey, G. Great to see you, G. See you later, G."

"That was weird," I say when he's gone.

Bob doesn't look up. "He's out to get you, you know."

"No kidding. Isn't Dallas out to get everyone?"

"Yeah. But you especially. Ever since you knocked him over in the gym."

"What? No one even saw that." But as I'm saying it I realize I must be wrong. Obviously, someone did.

"*Everyone* saw it. Anita, Chad, and Paul were like, high-fiving. He's been annoying them all year, calling them the Nerd Squad and asking Anita if she's going to get a perfect score on her SATs."

"The SATs? You mean for college?"

Bob is still drawing. "She thinks it's because she's Asian. *You* know. Like Asians are supposed to be super-smart or whatever."

I wonder if I'm wrong about Jason. Maybe he has changed, if he's willing to sit near a guy like Dallas at lunch every day.

"Speaking of the letter G," Bob says, "did you know that Benjamin Franklin wanted to get rid of it?"

"No kidding."

"Yeah. Not get rid of it totally. He wanted to keep the hard G and get rid of the soft G. You know, the hard G, as in *go*. And the soft G, like in *Georges*."

"Wouldn't that make George Washington really mad?"

"Well, he had plans for the soft G. He could have spelled it with a *J*, right? Except that *J* is one of the six letters he totally threw away."

"He threw out six letters?"

"Yeah. But he invented six new ones. He invented this letter *ish*, which sounds like *sh* and looks like a lowercase *H*, except with a swirly top. He wanted to blend the *ish* with other letters to get certain sounds. So he made the soft G sound by blending the *D* and the *ish*. It's a little confusing. And your name actually has a soft G at the beginning *and* the end, so it would look like this—"

He scribbles in the corner of his notebook and slides it over: *Dhordh*.

"Dehorda?"

"No," he says, "you have to think of the *ish* as 'sh.'"

"Shorsh?"

"You're not saying the *D*."

"Deshord-sha?"

"Are you even trying?"

"I thought the whole idea was to make it *not* confusing," I say.

"Yeah. But first you have to get used to it."

I don't point out how that's exactly the way regular spelling is. It may be weird sometimes, but you get used to it. I look at what Bob wrote, and I wonder: if Benjamin Franklin had his way, would Ms. Warner try to make everyone call me *ish*?

Bob English has his head down again. Then he passes me a note:

No ofens.

He sees me staring at it. "No offense," he whispers.

Last period. Gym.

Volleyball! Again.

Ms. Warner is standing just inside the gym doors with a big smile on her face as we all troop in.

"Really?" I ask her. "More volleyball?" She holds up her hand for a high five, but I leave her hanging because it's not Friday.

"Just try to have fun, G. Only two days till the weekend.

Remember, we're in this together." She looks sympathetic, but I'm beginning to wonder.

Dallas and Carter are right behind me. Again. Three steps past Ms. Warner and they start.

"Yeah, G. Try to have fun."

Ignore.

One of them squeezes my shoulder. "Big muscle, Gorgeous. I guess that's where the awesome serve comes from."

Ignore.

Carter says, "Hey, Gorgeous, I'm talking to you. Answer me. Is the big muscle where the awesome serve comes from?"

Dallas says, "Lay off him, Carter. You know freaks aren't good at sports."

Ignore.

After school, I catch Safer's call on the first ring. I've even had time to grab a pudding from the fridge.

"You're welcome," Safer says.

"For what?"

"I fixed your lock."

It hits me—for the first time, I didn't have to wrestle with my key.

"Hey, thanks."

"We have a problem. How soon can you get here?"

I eat my pudding on the stairs, glancing down at Mr. X's doormat on the way.

The gum wrapper is lying there, looking like an innocent piece of garbage. According to what Safer said last night, that means Mr. X is home. At least, I think that's what it means. I lean down and pick it up, hoping he doesn't choose that particular moment to open his door. But as usual, I don't hear a thing.

On six, Candy answers the bell and says, "You have chocolate on your chin."

"I forgot a spoon," I say, rubbing my face.

She walks me down the hall, as usual. When she's gone, I present the gum wrapper to Safer, who's on his knees, frowning through the window.

"Oh," he says. "So I guess you-know-who is home." But he seems distracted.

"What's wrong?" I ask him, dropping into my green beanbag.

"The parrots are in trouble. Something is definitely weird over there. The nest looks different. Smaller. And sort of—disrupted."

"Is that bad? Maybe they're downsizing. Or redecorating. My dad says knowing what to throw away is the single most important thing about sprucing up your home."

"That's not funny."

"Sorry. I thought it was a little funny. Maybe not *America's Funniest Home Videos* funny, but, you know, a *modicum* of funny. That's a vocabulary word. You probably don't know about those."

He turns around to stare at me. "What's with you today?"

I shrug.

"Do me a favor," Safer says. "Go downstairs and check the sidewalk under the nest. See if there are any sticks down there."

"Sticks," I repeat. I'm so comfortable in the beanbag.

"Yeah, sticks. Just go check it out, okay?"

"Why can't you check it out?"

"I'm watching from up here!"

What I want to say is "Watching what, exactly?" But I say, "Fine, I'll go," and pull myself out of my beanbag.

In the elevator I imagine a bird decorator who's wearing my dad's glasses—the funky rectangular ones he wears when he has a meeting—and flipping through a bird-size binder full of twig samples.

There actually *are* a bunch of little sticks on the sidewalk across the street, and one green feather. It's creepy, like I'm looking at a crime scene. I take the feather back to Safer, who holds it thoughtfully.

"I wonder if there was an attack on the nest," he says. "It happens sometimes."

"Who would want to attack some parrots? They have nothing worth taking."

Safer looks at me like I'm nuts. "You're joking, right? I'm not talking about a robbery. I'm talking about falcons or hawks—don't they teach you about birds of prey at school?"

Well, no. They don't.

Safer is staring out the window again, running the feather up and down one arm.

"Whoa!" Candy has crept up on us. Her pig slippers should be standard-issue spyware. They are that quiet. "Please tell me that's not a real feather."

"It came from—" I point through the window at the parrots' nest.

Candy shouts at Safer, "Are you trying to give us all avian

flu? Put that down! Throw it away! And—take a shower, for Pete's sake!" She stomps away in near silence.

"Her stomping will be a lot more effective when she outgrows those slippers," I say.

He ignores me. "After an attack, survivors usually flee the nest. I bet they're gone. All we can do is wait to see if they come back."

"Maybe we should watch the lobbycam for a while," I say.

Which perks him right up.

Bounce and Yank

I'm trying to imitate Safer's infuriating talent for focusing his full attention on a tile floor and a locked glass door, but every time I set my eyes on that little black-and-white screen, my mind starts to wander away and I have to bring it back.

I miss Mom all of a sudden, like the feeling has been there all along and I can't ignore it anymore. It's like that buzzing sound I heard in the lobby on the morning we moved, right before Safer came down with the dogs, and how I was hearing that sound before I even knew I was hearing it.

Then I realize that I know what that buzzing sound *was* on the morning we moved, and I turn and look at Safer in surprise. He doesn't move his eyes from the screen, but he says, "What?"

I'm about to say, "You were watching me that first day when I moved in. You were watching me through the lobby-cam. It buzzes, you know. Like static." But I don't. I decide I want to think about whether to say this to him.

"Nothing," I say.

And then I remember to put my brain back on the screen, where it wanders away again, this time to Dad.

The night Dad told us he got laid off, Mom said that if anyone knew how to bounce back it was Dad. They sat together on the couch and talked about all the other stuff he'd always wanted to do with his life, like start his business where he helps people make their houses look old. He got out his leather-covered notepad with the graph paper that Mom bought him for Christmas one year, and he started making a list of potential clients, and Mom rubbed his shoulders. Later, when I was brushing my teeth, I heard them talking in their bedroom.

"Remember those extra shifts they offered me at work?" Mom said.

"The ones with the crazy hours?" Dad said.

"And the excellent pay. I'm going to call them in the morning."

"You hate the night shift," Dad said.

"I do not."

Which was when I realized that Dad's getting laid off was more serious than they were pretending it was.

Bounce, I think.

"Bounce?" Safer says.

Oops. Sometimes I say a word out loud without knowing it. Certain kinds of words more than others.

"*Bounce* is a weird word," I say.

"Weird how?"

"It's like—it sounds the same as what it is."

He tries it. "Bounce."

"Bounce," I repeat.

"You're right," Safer says.

No one talks for a minute. We watch the screen and I do not let my mind wander.

"You know what's another word like that?" Safer says.

"What?"

"*Yank.*"

Yank, I think. *Yank.* I say out it loud: "Yank. Yeah, that works."

I'm wondering how many people in the world would have understood right away what I meant about the word *bounce,* the way Safer just did.

Absolutely nothing is happening on the intercom screen. It's a picture of an empty lobby. Safer says he trusts me to keep an eye on it while he gets us some peanut butter crackers.

"The thing about Mr. X," he says, handing me three cracker sandwiches, "is that he's careful. So observation will only get us so far."

"What do you think he's doing that's so bad?" I ask. "You never actually said."

"I have a few working theories."

"Like?"

"You don't want to know."

"But *shouldn't* I know?"

"I'm afraid you'll get upset."

"I won't."

"Okay. Ask yourself this question: Why would someone carry suitcases out of his apartment all the time? Heavy ones?"

"I don't know."

"Because you aren't thinking. Think: people in, suitcases out."

"You think he's chopping people up and putting them in the suitcases?"

He looks at me and raises his eyebrows. "You said it, I didn't."

"Okay, *that* is nuts."

"Is it?"

"Do you even see people going into his apartment? You said, 'People in, suitcases out.' But what people are going in?"

"Hard to know—people get buzzed in all the time. Who's to say where they're going?"

"Who's to say they're being chopped up into little pieces!"

"Exactly," Safer says. "That's why we need evidence!"

I'm just sitting there, what they call dumbstruck. "I've never even seen the guy," I manage to say.

Safer nods. "You're still developing your lobbycam stamina." He looks at his watch. "I have to walk the dogs. You coming?"

I'm trying to act less freaked out than I feel. I can't decide if he's serious.

"I told you you'd be upset," Safer says. "You didn't listen."

Safer's dog walking is mostly a lunchtime job. That's when he takes four of them at once. People walk their own dogs after work, he tells me, except for one guy who works late and one lady who just had a baby. Safer walks their dogs, Ty and Lucky, twice a day, and sometimes on the weekend.

Safer knocks on 2A. I hear a baby crying somewhere far away behind the door.

"Who is it?" a voice says.

"It's me—Safer."

"Who?"

"Safer!"

"Whoooo?"

"Hey!" I say. "Is that the moo-cow kid?"

Safer just glares at the door. A few seconds later, there's a knock from inside the apartment.

"Who's there?" Safer asks.

"Interrupting cow!"

"Interrupting cow wh—"

"Moo! MOOOOOO!"

Safer rolls his eyes at me, but the door is finally being unlocked, and a giant yellow dog comes bounding out, knocking Safer off balance so that he has to grab the wall or fall down. He gives Lucky a hug—a hug like you'd give a person.

Lucky is one of those incredibly slobbery dogs, with slime leaking over black lips at the corners of her mouth. Now Safer is letting her lick his face all over, and I'm thinking that if he doesn't get a bird disease, he'll probably get a dog disease.

The moo-cow kid is holding out Lucky's leash, being helpful for once. "And here's the poop bag!" he says, shoving a crumpled plastic bag at me.

I put both hands up and say, "No thanks."

Safer grabs it and stuffs it into his pocket.

"Babies are so stupid," the moo-cow kid says. "They don't even know where we hang the leash. And they don't wear *shoes*." He slams the door on us.

* * *

We collect Ty, which is easy because Safer just lets himself into the guy's empty apartment with one of the keys on his giant key ring, and then we head down the stairs to the basement, where Safer unwedges a grimy Spalding pinky ball from behind a big pipe that runs along the wall. A metal door leads into the courtyard.

Standing in the courtyard is kind of like being a mouse at the bottom of a concrete garbage can, high walls all around and daylight up there somewhere. Safer starts throwing the ball for the dogs to fetch. They take turns bringing it back, very civilized. Whenever Lucky gets the ball, I let Safer deal with the slobber. I can handle Ty, though, because he's not a big spitter.

When the dogs do their business and Safer cleans up after them, I don't watch. He takes the plastic bags I'm not looking at and heads inside to throw them away.

As soon as he disappears into the basement, the dogs sort of deflate. They both stop playing and stare at the door.

"He's coming right back," I tell them. "He just went to throw away your—bags." They give me a quick glance, and then it's back to staring down the door with these worried-eyebrow looks. I never even noticed before this that dogs *have* eyebrows.

When Safer reappears, Ty and Lucky act like it's a miracle. They're leaping all over the place, practically hugging each other, and putting both paws up on Safer's legs like they need to touch him to know he's real.

"Geez," I say. "I *told* them you were coming right back."

"Come inside," Safer says. "I have to show you something."

Fieldwork

"Over here," Safer says, jerking his head toward the laundry room, where he strolls around, very casual. "Notice anything unusual?"

Besides the washers and dryers, a couple of which are running, there are gray concrete walls, a wobbly table, a big metal sink, and a red plastic laundry basket.

"No."

"Because you aren't *looking*," Safer says.

"I *am* looking!"

"Check out the dryers again."

"I see—dryers. One has clothes going around and around. Getting dry."

He looks at the ceiling with an expression that says he is trying to be patient. "But what *about* the clothes?"

And I *do* see.

"Black!" I shout, pointing at the middle dryer. "The clothes in there are all black!"

"Shhhhh."

"Sorry." I keep forgetting that the number-one rule of spying is *don't yell*.

But Safer looks pleased. "It's time for some field training. You're going to go through those clothes and see what there is to see."

"What?"

"I'll be your lookout," he says.

"You mean take some guy's sopping wet clothes out of the dryer and—and what?"

"And go through the pockets. No biggie."

"No biggie? No *way*."

"Fine. I'll do it. You be *my* lookout." Which I get the feeling was his plan all along.

Safer posts me in the little hallway between the laundry room and the elevator. I'm not watching the stairs because Safer is pretty sure he's the only person who ever uses them.

I hear the sound of the dryer stopping, like a little sigh, and I glance up at the arrow above the elevator. It's resting at *L*, for lobby, just sitting there, so I step away and peek into the laundry room.

Safer's moving fast, grabbing armfuls of black clothes and throwing them onto the Formica table. When the dryer is empty, he shoves his pile to one side of the table, grabs something—a pair of pants—and checks the pockets. Which can't be easy, because they look pretty wet.

He looks up, calm as can be, and says, "Georges, the elevator is moving."

I rush out and see that he's right. It's on three already, still going up. I watch the arrow move . . . 4 . . . 5 . . . it stops on 6.

"It stopped on six!" I call to Safer, because that's his floor, but he doesn't answer.

I hear the motor start up again and keep my eye on the arrow: 6 . . . 5 . . . 4 . . .

It stops on 4. Mr. X's floor. And if that's Mr. X's laundry . . .

"It stopped on four!" I shout.

"Stay calm," Safer replies. "Spies don't freak out."

"It's moving again!"

. . . 3 . . . 2 . . . L.

It doesn't stop on L.

It's coming to the basement.

"It's coming down!" I yell. "To the basement!"

Safer calls back one word: "Stall!"

Stall? I'm going to look like an idiot just standing there staring when the elevator door opens. I quick open one of the garbage cans behind me and grab a bag of garbage. It's wet from something that spatters my leg below my shorts. I hold tight to the top of the bag and wait.

It's only when the elevator door begins to open that it occurs to me that waiting in the basement with a bag of garbage makes absolutely no sense. Waiting with a bag of garbage to go *to* the basement, yes. But waiting for the elevator *in* the basement, not so much. I quickly step away from the bag, which is now leaking all over the floor. And smelling kind of bad. Maybe it'll just be Candy, I tell myself.

It isn't Candy. And it isn't Mr. X. It's Safer's mom.

"Oh, hi, Georges. I'm looking for Safer. Is he down here?"

"Hi! Um, I'm not sure. I think so. He might be."

She looks at me funny.

"Is that your garbage, Georges? It's leaking. Better get it into a can."

"That? No! I just saw it here. Just now."

She blinks. "Oh. How strange."

This is not going well at all. "You know what?" I say. "I was just thinking I should put it into a can. That's what I was doing—standing here, thinking that. Because it's leaking."

"Yes, it is. I think I just said that." She starts to move past me.

"But then I was thinking, what if someone is coming back for it?"

She stops. "Coming back," she repeats. "For—the garbage."

"Yeah! But that's dumb, isn't it? I'll throw it away right now." I open the same garbage can I took the bag out of, which is a mistake because the bottom of the can is covered with the same gucky brown stuff that's leaking out of the bag, which, if you are a person who likes to analyze things, might suggest that the bag had actually been in there before.

But Safer's mom doesn't ask me about that, because right then the dogs both start barking up a storm in the courtyard. They want Safer.

"Didn't you come down here with Safer to walk the dogs?" She points to the courtyard door. "Is he outside?"

"Um. He *was*. . . ."

Safer comes walking out of the laundry room. "Hi, Mom." He holds up two wet hands. "Just washing up. After the dogs."

"Good idea," she says. "Listen, can you stay upstairs with Candy for a little while? I have to run an errand."

"Sure. I just have to drop off Ty and Lucky." He looks at me. "Coming?"

"Yeah. I have to stop by my apartment first, though."
Because my leg is covered in smelly brown gook.

I get in the elevator with Safer's mom, and Safer waves goodbye to us, smiling through the little glass window in the elevator door.

Safer's mom stares at my sneakers with a funny expression until we get to the lobby. "You're welcome to join us for dinner, Georges," she says when the door opens. "It's Candy's night to cook."

"Candy cooks dinner?"

"Why not? I believe she's planning to make peanut butter and bananas on hot dog buns."

"Um, that sounds good. But I should check with my dad."

She nods. "And maybe change your socks, while you're at it."

I look down and see that one of my socks has that brown garbage juice all over it. I look up to say something, but the door is already closing.

The phone is ringing before I can get my sneakers off. Safer is very fast on those stairs.

"I have something to show you," Safer says. "Come right away."

"I kind of freaked out back there," I tell him. "I think your mom noticed."

"My mom is a very accepting person," Safer says. "Don't worry about it. Just come up right away."

"As soon as I wash my leg."

"Did you say you're washing your legs?"

"Never mind."

* * *

Upstairs, Safer is in his beanbag chair with a big smile on his face. He holds up a little gold-colored key.

"Seriously? *That* was in the dryer?"

"Pants pocket," he says. He tosses the key to me, first doing a couple of fakes so I know it's coming, but I still miss and have to pick it up off the floor. At least he doesn't laugh.

It's a funny little key. It looks like it should open a miniature treasure chest. "I can't believe you found this."

"Now we just have to figure out what it opens."

I think Safer pictures a little box of evil in a corner of Mr. X's apartment, and he thinks that if he can find it, he'll save the world, or at least a small part of Brooklyn.

And who am I to say that he's wrong?

"We've got to get inside," Safer says.

"Inside Mr. X's apartment."

He nods. "Exactly. Tomorrow."

"Tomorrow?" I say. "*Tomorrow* tomorrow?"

My cell phone rings. "My dad," I tell Safer, flipping it open. And that's when I remember that I was supposed to meet Dad downstairs at five o'clock to go to the orthodontist.

"Sorry!" I tell him. "Be right down."

"I can't stay for dinner," I tell Safer.

"Were you staying for dinner?" Candy appears in the doorway. She must have bat ears or something. Either that or she was standing in the hall, listening. "No one even bothered to tell me! I would have bought more bananas!"

"That's okay," I tell her. "I really have to go. I have an orthodontist's appointment."

"Really? Is your orthodontist in the city?"

"Yeah."

"Will you be taking the D train, by any chance?"

"Candy, *no,*" Safer says, hauling himself out of his beanbag.

"I'm just *asking.*"

"I'm not sure," I tell her. "Why?"

"There's a newsstand on the uptown D platform at Fifty-Ninth Street that sells giant SweeTarts. They're really hard to find around here." Her eyes look all lit up. It's like she's glowing.

"If you *happen* to be there," she says, glancing at Safer, "and you *happen* to see them, would you buy two packs for me? I'll pay you back. I have the money. I can show you the money right now."

"That's okay," I say. "I believe you."

"And let me know if you're ever going to Yankee Stadium," she says. "I got Lemonheads at a store near Yankee Stadium once."

"Lemonheads?"

"You can hardly ever find them. I saved the box. Do you want to see the box?"

"He's leaving now!" Safer yells at her, pulling me down the hall. "He doesn't want to see the stupid Lemonheads box!"

Actually, I'm kind of curious. But I *am* late, and so I let him drag me to the door.

"*Tomorrow,*" he says, and he shoves a fresh gum wrapper into my hand.

That night I try to fall asleep before my teeth start aching from the tightened braces. We didn't take the D train after all: Dad drove Mom's car into the city, and we must have both been feeling quiet, because we hardly talked at all. When we got home I pretended that the garbage was full and said I would take it down to the basement. While I was waiting for the elevator, I ran up to Mr. X's and shoved the gum wrapper between his door and the doorframe. When I got back to the apartment, Dad was already shut up in his room with the door closed.

I get out of bed and spell Mom a note:

OUCH TEETH
LOVE ME

I dream about Ty and Lucky, with their worried-eyebrow looks, staring at that metal door.

Big Picture

Bob English passes me a note in science:

Ghoti.

"Say it," he says.

"Go-tee," I read.

He shakes his head. "Wrong. It says *fish*."

"Um, it definitely does not say *fish*."

"Sure it does." He leans forward to point. "*G-h* as in the word *laugh*, *o* as in *women*, and *t-i* as in *nation*. See? *Fish*."

My teeth are aching. Mom's morning Scrabble note said ADVIL, but I couldn't find any. I tell Bob sorry, I didn't quite follow that, which is a mistake because he spells it all out for me in another note:

> gh = as in the word laugh (f sound)
> o = as in the word women (i sound)
> ti = as in the word nation (sh sound)

"Okay, now I get it," I say.

"I'm just demonstrating the absurdity of English spelling."

"But that's not the English spelling. It's spelled *f-i-s-h*."

Bob sticks his hand into his Sharpie bag and flicks through the pens until he finds the one he wants. "Sure it is. If you want to play the game the way everyone else does."

Bob English is making less and less sense. But I like him more and more.

Lunch. Tacos. School taco shells smell like plastic, so I drag my tray down to the bagel basket, where Dallas and Carter immediately show up and then pretend they don't see me.

Dallas bumps me with one shoulder and acts surprised. "Oh, man! Sorry. I didn't see you, geek. I mean, *Georges*."

And they walk away, chanting "Geek, geek, geek, geek."

Typical bully crap, Mom would say. *Big picture.*

I think about Sir Ott, hanging over the couch at home, and how much I would like to be there right now, kicking back with some *America's Funniest Home Videos*.

And then I think of all those thousands of dots Seurat used to paint the picture. I think about how if you stand back from the painting, you can see the people, the green grass and that cute monkey on a leash, but if you get closer, the monkey kind of dissolves right in front of your eyes. Like Mom says, life is a million different dots making one gigantic picture. And maybe the big picture is nice, maybe it's amazing, but if you're standing with your face pressed up against a bunch of black dots, it's really hard to tell.

After school, I watch *America's Funniest Home Videos* and let the phone ring. It rings and stops, rings and stops, but no one leaves a message on the machine.

The third time it starts, I grab the remote and pause the show. It's one of my favorites: this very serious-looking little girl is sitting in a high chair and counting from one to ten for her grandmother, who isn't paying attention and doesn't realize that what the girl is really doing is sticking these baked beans up her nose. "One . . . two . . . three . . ."

"Where were you?" Safer asks. "We have work to do. Don't forget to check the you-know-what on your way up."

I start up the stairs, glancing in my most casual spylike way at Mr. X's doormat as I pass it. But there's no gum wrapper on the mat—it's still stuck in the doorframe.

On six, Candy answers the door.

"So is it your official job to answer the door?" I ask her while we walk down the long hallway to the living room.

"Pretty much," she says. "Pigeon's at practice, Dad's at work, and Mom's busy touching up the photos from last weekend's wedding."

"What about Safer?"

"Ha!" she says. "Good one."

Safer's mom calls to us from her office, where she's looking at a picture on a computer screen. It's a woman's head, blown up to twice the size of a normal head.

"What do you think?" she asks. "Too many flyaways? I want it to look natural."

"Looks good to me," Candy says.

"What's a flyaway?" I ask.

"Hair—see how her hair is blowing around a little? They got married on a dock, the wind was crazy. I'm erasing some of the flying hair because it's a distraction, but I don't want to go too far and remove the illusion of movement, you know?"

I don't notice anything about the woman's hair. What I notice is that she has something green stuck between her teeth.

"Oh, I know," Safer's mom says. "That's broccoli. It's next on my list."

"Are you supposed to make everyone look perfect?" I ask her.

"It's part of the deal," she says. "Believe it or not, you probably won't want broccoli in your teeth in your wedding pictures either."

"I wouldn't care if there was something green in my teeth," Candy says. "I think it would be kind of funny. And Mr. Orange won't care either, I bet."

"Who?" I ask.

"Mr. Orange. That's who I'm going to marry. Someone who likes orange."

"You're going to marry someone because you both like orange?"

"No!" She makes a face. "I hate orange. The color *and* the flavor. It's the only flavor I don't like, actually. That's the whole point. I hate it, he loves it. That way we can always share the pack."

"Pack of what?"

"Starbursts. Lifesavers. Jolly Ranchers. Whatever."

"Are you kidding?" I glance at Safer's mom, but she's obviously heard this before, and has moved on to the broccoli-teeth problem.

"Why would I be kidding?" Candy says. "I've decided that

the whole getting-married thing is kind of random anyway. You know how many times my grandparents met before they got married? Once! They met on a train, and that was it. You should see how much they still love each other!"

"But—"

"And my friend Joanie from fencing told me her parents went out for like ten years before they got married. And guess what? They got divorced like a year and a half later! So I'm going to make it very simple."

She's almost making sense.

"I mean, he'll have to be cute and everything," she says.

I nod.

"Not like, *television* cute. Real-person cute. Like . . . a real person."

"I guess candy is pretty important to you," I say.

She laughs. "You think? I mean, why do you think my name is Candy!"

"Or maybe you like Candy because your *name* is Candy," I say. "Ever think of that?"

She stops smiling. "No. That makes no sense."

Her mom turns to me. "She has it the right way around, actually. Because we let the kids name themselves."

"When they were—babies?"

"Not babies, exactly. But by age two or so they had expressed who they were and what they cared about most. We just sort of—interpreted."

She looks completely serious.

Candy nods. "I've been obsessed with candy since birth, practically. And same with Pigeon and—pigeons."

"All birds, actually," her mom says. "But pigeons are

mostly what we have in Brooklyn." She laughs and looks at Candy. "And just think. If we had named you at birth, we might have called you Orange! What a disaster that would have been."

I'm wondering whether to tell Mom this story. It might knock Safer's whole family back from "smart bohemians" to "nice bohemians."

"Are you named after anyone?" Candy asks me.

"Actually, yeah—my parents love this artist named Seurat. His first name was Georges. With an *s*."

"Your name has an *s*?" Candy says. "That's cool. Like a secret letter or something."

Safer's mom smiles. "Oh, I love Seurat." The way she says "Seurat" is funny—it's like she starts gargling in the middle of it. And she forgets the *T*, so it's "Sir"—gargle—"ahh." I wonder if this is the way actual French people say it.

She turns to Candy. "His color theory was amazing. Instead of using purple, he would put a dab of red next to a dab of blue, and together the colors would be *perceived* as purple. In the mind of the viewer. Isn't that incredible?"

"Yeah, all the dots," I say. "He was kind of part artist, part scientist, I guess, just like my parents—my dad is the artist type, and my mom is the scientist type. They actually met in a class called Physics for Poets. In college."

Then Safer's mom says, "I can't wait to meet your mom, Georges."

"Hey!" Safer is standing in the doorway. "What happened to you?"

"Oh—sorry. I got sidetracked."

"I was telling him about our names," Candy says.

Safer glances at his mom. "*Whose* names?"

"Mine," Candy says. "And Pigeon's. Don't worry, I didn't—"

Safer interrupts her. "Candy, will you just go away, please?"

"I'm the one who answered the door! You know that ding-dong sound you hear sometimes? That's the doorbell!"

"Fine," he tells her. "Just go away."

"Safer," his mom says. "This is my office. I'm the only one who can tell her to go away."

"Fine." He grabs my arm. "Let's go, Georges."

When we're in our beanbag chairs, Safer holds out his flask. "Coffee?"

"So why *are* you called Safer? Your mom says you guys named yourselves."

He waves the flask impatiently. "Not exactly. Look, we're wasting time. We need to get into Mr. X's apartment. To see what the key opens. I have a feeling it's important."

"I'm not going into anyone's apartment," I say.

"One step at a time," he says. "Is the gum wrapper still in the door?"

I admit that it is.

"Great," Safer says. "He's not home yet. I have a plan."

Safer's plan is that I will watch the lobbycam in my apartment while he breaks into Mr. X's apartment right above me. If I see Mr. X coming in through the lobby, which he says is "highly doubtful," I will bang SOS on the heating pipe that runs through my kitchen—and through the kitchen of Mr. X.

Safer will hear the banging and run up to his own apartment before Mr. X gets in and murders him.

When I remind Safer that I haven't ever actually *seen* Mr. X, he tells me not to worry, that I will recognize him because he is the only person who wears all black in May.

"But how are you going to get into his apartment?" I ask. "Isn't it locked?"

"Not everyone locks their doors," Safer says thoughtfully.

The next thing I know we're standing in front of Mr. X's apartment. It's the first time I really stop and look at his door. I haven't noticed the three stickers under the peephole—one for the ASPCA, one that says *Eat Meat Without Feet,* and one that says *Support the Audubon Society.*

"Go ahead, try it," Safer says.

"Try what?"

"The doorknob."

"What? No *way.*"

"I already told you, he's not here." He points to the gum wrapper, still stuck in the doorframe.

What I Still Don't Totally Get About the Gum Wrapper Business

According to Safer:

I stick the gum wrapper in Mr. X's door at night, when Mr. X is home.

When Mr. X leaves his apartment in the morning, the door opens and the wrapper falls out.

Safer checks the door every half-hour starting early

in the morning. When he sees that the wrapper is out, he knows that Mr. X has gone out, and Safer puts the wrapper back in the doorframe so we'll know when Mr. X comes back in.

As long as it stays there, Mr. X is still *out*. It should be safe to enter the apartment as long as someone is the lookout on the lobbycam, watching to see if Mr. X comes into the building.

But I wonder:

What if Mr. X is *out* when I put the wrapper in at night, so the wrapper is actually falling out when he comes *in*, and then Safer replaces it in the morning, when Mr. X is *still in*. In other words, *who knows?*

—or—

What if he *is* home when I put the wrapper in the door at night, and the wrapper does fall out when Mr. X leaves in the morning, but then he *comes back* within the same half-hour? Like maybe he just went for a *bagel*.

Again, Safer would replace the wrapper in the door while he's *home*.

Which would mean that right now, with both of us standing on Mr. X's doormat looking at the wrapper in the door, Mr. X could actually be *home* or *not home*.

Either one.

umami

When I blurt all of this out on Mr. X's doormat, Safer gives me a look and says that if I keep going down this road, I will be "paralyzed by my own logic."

"Relax," he tells me. "I know what I'm doing."

"I'm not touching that door," I say.

"Fine." Safer's hand shoots out and jiggles the doorknob. Locked.

He turns and sprints back up to his apartment, and I follow, thinking about how turning someone else's doorknob is such a small thing but also such a creepy thing.

"It was worth a shot," Safer says, writing in his notebook. "And now we know he doesn't bolt it. He just uses the slam-lock."

"How can you tell?"

"It's the way the knob wiggles—you get to know these things."

Safer picks up the binoculars and looks through the window.

"Safer," I say.

"Yeah?"

"What would you have done if the door hadn't been locked?"

He lowers the binoculars and looks at me. "I would have made a note of it. It would have been an important fact."

"So you weren't about to walk in there, right? Into the guy's apartment?"

"What do you think I am? An amateur? I would never just barge in without a plan, Georges. Planning is essential. That's why we observe habits, reactions, everything. This is what I've been trying to teach you."

He turns back to the window and raises the binoculars. "People are not so different from birds, you know. If you watch them long enough, you find out everything you need to know."

"Are the parrots back yet?" I squint out the window toward the nest.

"Not yet. Give them a couple of— *Candy, what do you want?*"

Candy is standing just inside the living room, holding a piece of paper. Safer must have eyes in the back of his head.

She ignores Safer and holds the paper out to me. "I printed this out for you," she tells me. "It's about umami—remember the other night, you told us about how there's this fifth taste?—anyway, it's kind of interesting. This guy in Japan was obsessed with the idea of discovering the fifth taste, because he knew there had to be more than four, but no one really believed him, or, um, cared, I guess. So he boiled down all this seaweed and got to this deep flavor that isn't sweet or salty or sour or bitter. It's some glutamate thing that they put in Chinese food. Anyway, that's the fifth taste. It's also in mushrooms." She thrusts the paper at me.

"Wow," I say. "Thanks."

"It's all in there—and by the way, *umami* means 'deliciousness,' even though I don't remotely like mushrooms."

I look down at the article and see that she has underlined most of the sentences. "Thanks," I tell her again.

She starts to walk away, then stops. "It doesn't really make sense. Delicious totally depends on the person eating the food."

I nod. "Yeah, I've thought about that. Why don't we all like the same foods? Shouldn't we be sort of programmed to eat anything that's good for us? And to spit out anything that's poison? You know, from evolution?"

"Yeah," she says. "Like, why do I hate orange? Obviously if I was a cavewoman and I found some orange trees, I should eat the oranges, right? Who knows when I would find food again?"

"Yeah." I say. It's kind of funny to picture Candy as a cavewoman wearing those pig slippers.

"I really do hate oranges, though. I can't even sit across from someone drinking orange juice."

"Weird."

Safer is staring at us.

"What?"

"Nothing," he says. "Georges, weren't you about to ask me downstairs? To help you look for that *key*? Not that it isn't fascinating about the oranges and the seaweed."

* * *

Five minutes later, Safer is standing in my kitchen with a knife in his hand. "Remember, SOS is easy: three quick, three slow, three quick."

Holding the knife by the wrong end, he uses the handle to beat the rhythm against the heating pipe that runs from the floor to the ceiling:

Tap-tap-tap . . . tap, tap, tap . . . tap-tap-tap.

"Now you," he says, holding out the knife.

"Why SOS?" I ask. "I mean, I could just bang on the pipe, right? You'd know it was me."

"Banging on the pipe is sloppy. It could mean anything. It could be Mr. Gervais complaining about the heat."

"In May?"

Safer fixes me with one his looks. "Who's training who, Georges?"

I take the knife and give it a try: *Tap-tap-tap. Tap . . . tap . . . tap. Tap-tap-tap.*

"Harder," Safer says. "Remember, I have to hear this upstairs. I can barely hear it standing right next to you."

"You still haven't figured out how to get in. Shouldn't that be number one on the agenda?"

Safer takes an American Express card out of his back pocket. "This is how I'm getting in."

"You're going to pay someone to open the door?"

"Don't be stupid, Georges. It's expired. Mr. X doesn't bolt his door, remember? For the slam-lock, this is all I need. I just shove it in that crack between the door and the frame"—he cuts down through the air with the arm holding the card— "and voilà."

"You've done this before?" I guess I finally know how Safer left me that note under my pillow.

Safer looks at me scornfully. "Of course."

Maybe Safer has no conscience at all.

"I'm not sure we should do this," I say. Because I'm sure we shouldn't do this.

"It's normal to be a little scared, Georges."

"I'm not scared." Though it has crossed my mind that a person could go to jail for the kind of thing Safer is planning.

"Fine, I'll go in without a lookout. But if he finds me in there, he'll probably kill me. I just want you to know that."

"That's exactly why I'm telling you not to do it."

"I don't expect you to understand, because you just moved in. But something has been going on with this guy for a while. The visitors, the suitcases . . ."

"What *visitors*? You don't even know if there *were* any visitors."

He shakes his head. "Spies don't speculate."

I don't say anything.

"It's not as if you'll be exposed," he says. "You'll be right here, in your own apartment. Please, Georges? It would be nice not to go in there naked."

"Naked? Why would you be naked?"

He blows his cheeks out. "Not *actually* naked. *Naked* means going in with no backup, no cover."

I give up. "I'll be your lookout this *one* time. And maybe you'll find out there's nothing going on at all. Maybe Mr. X isn't a murderer."

He smiles. "Remember, three quick, three slow, three

quick." He stands up and shoves the credit card into his back pocket. "See? It's not so scary, Georges. Not so scary at all."

But it is scary.

"When?"

He smiles. "*Now*, Georges. Try to keep up."

Break and Enter (#1)

"I'll think I'll leave my shoes here," Safer says. "Do you mind? I don't want to track anything in, and I don't want to leave them by Mr. X's door. If I have to leave in a hurry I might forget them. And then he'd find them, and he'd start looking for a boy about my size, and—"

"It's fine," I say. "Leave them."

He unties his sneakers and steps out of them. "Okay, so it's three—"

"Three quick, three slow, three quick," I say. "Got it."

"If I'm not back in ten minutes, it means something is very wrong," Safer says.

"And what am I supposed to do then?"

"Call the police, I guess."

"Are you serious? What if you wipe out in your socks on the bathroom floor up there, hit your head on the bathtub, and pass out, and then I call the police, and we have to explain what you were doing up there in the first place? We could both go to jail!"

He stares at me. Then he bends down, takes off his socks,

and tosses them on top of his sneakers. "If I'm not back in ten minutes, call the police because it means I have not slipped in the bathroom in my socks and I am most likely in the vise-like grip of a raving lunatic. Okay?"

I nod.

Then he shakes my hand very formally and walks out the door.

I rush over to the lobbycam and push the button. The lobby door flickers into view on the screen. I grip my butter knife. I have this pins-and-needles feeling in my legs, like it's me who's forcing open the door of a stranger's apartment, walking in, looking, touching. It's the same feeling I get when Dad and I fly kites at the Cape, as if holding on to the string means that part of me is up there, way too high.

I watch the clock. Every two minutes, the screen turns itself off and I push the button to make the picture come back.

Absolutely nothing happens for six minutes, except that I have pushed the View button three times. The pins-and-needles feeling is gone, and I wish I had brought a chair to sit on.

Then, finally, there's some action. The moo-cow kid comes into the lobby with his teenage babysitter, who's wearing a pair of headphones and fumbling in her backpack—for her keys, I'm guessing. The moo-cow kid isn't spinning around or anything. He actually looks a little sad.

I push the Talk button on the intercom and say, "Knock, knock."

The teenager ignores me, probably she can't even hear

anything with those headphones on, but the moo-cow kid's mouth falls open. He's looking all around. "Who's there?" he asks the ceiling.

"Interrupting kangaroo," I say.

He breaks into this huge smile. "Interrupting kangaroo wh—"

"Kanga-ROO! Kanga-ROO!" I shout, because I have no idea what sound a kangaroo actually makes.

The moo-cow kid is cracking up. His babysitter has found her keys, and they walk through the door. Then the lobby is empty again.

"Having fun?"

I whirl around and there's Safer, leaning against the wall behind me with his arms crossed.

"It's a relief to know that you were worried about me," he says. "I mean, I could be bleeding to death from a head wound in Mr. X's bathroom and here you are, playing with the intercom."

I glance at the clock. "It's only been seven minutes. You took off your socks."

"And *you* have been here telling knock-knock jokes to the whole building!"

"Safer, do you really think that anyone who isn't *us* is standing around in front of their intercoms pressing the Talk button?"

"The number-one rule of the lobbycam is *silence*."

"You never said that."

"I didn't think I had to."

"So how did it go? Did you figure out what the key is for?"

He shakes his head. "I saw a couple of disturbing things up there, Georges. Very disturbing."

"Like what?"

Safer says he needs a minute. He wants to know if we have any potato chips, which we don't. He settles for a string cheese. I get him a glass of water, which he guzzles. Finally, he looks up at me.

"One word, Georges: *handsaw*."

Safer tells me:

One, Mr. X has a handsaw laid out on newspaper on his dining-room table, and it looks sharp; two, he has all sorts of bleach and cleansers under his kitchen sink; three, his bathtub is very clean—"too clean"; and four, Safer couldn't find anything that could be opened with the little gold key.

He needs to go home and think. He takes a string cheese for the road and doesn't invite me to come with him. After he goes, I look up *kangaroo* on Wikipedia and find out that kangaroos don't make a particular sound. Mostly they just thump with their feet to communicate.

I watch *America's Funniest Home Videos* until Dad gets home.

We go to Yum Li's.

Dad and I have the usual.

"Tell me things!" Dad says, just in case I'm in the mood to pour my heart out.

"Things," I say, cramming chicken and broccoli into my mouth.

So he tells me about another big potential client he might get, who's a friend of the first big potential client. This is called word of mouth, and he says it's good news for our summer vacation.

"I saw Mom this afternoon," he tells me. "She's a trouper, Georges. You know that about your mom, right? She's amazing. Really strong. Everything is going great over there."

"Good," I say. "That's . . . really good."

Dad's fortune says: *Only a goofus locks his keys in his car twice in one week.*

He looks injured. "I don't even have a car!"

Mine says: *It's a cookie, Sherlock.*

We're almost home when I see Candy, Pigeon, and their parents walking from the other direction. Candy is carrying a pizza box. Everyone stops to say hi, and then we all walk into the lobby together.

"DeMarco's?" I say to Candy, while the dads are introducing themselves.

She nods. "I was thinking that pizza must be umami. It's got tomatoes *and* Parmesan cheese. And it doesn't really fit any of the other categories."

"Definitely," I tell her. "So where's Safer?"

"Oh, this is for him." She raises the box. "We ate at the restaurant. Pigeon says DeMarco's pizza has a half-life of ten minutes. That's from chemistry, and it means he only eats it fresh out of the oven."

"So you're the famous Georges," Safer's dad says to me. I tell him I guess I am, and he makes a big deal out of shaking my hand. He's wearing a black polo shirt that has the words *Sixth Sense* embroidered on it. Nobody mentions Safer. I wonder if he didn't go to DeMarco's because he's still mad at Pigeon. Maybe he's one of those people who holds a grudge forever.

I watch some TV with Sir Ott while Dad goes up and down to the basement, doing late-night laundry. Mom calls while he's downstairs, and she sounds pretty tired. She says she could use a laugh and asks me to tell her about one of America's Funniest Home Videos, so I tell her about the girl sticking the beans up her nose, and Mom cracks up, which is actually good to hear. But then she says one of the doctors just walked in and she has to hang up.

When the laundry is dry, Dad sits next to me on the couch to fold, stacking everything on the coffee table in front of us. Dad's a very good folder. He can even make Mom's super-puffy bathrobe into a nice neat square. When he goes to the bathroom I plant my face in it and inhale. But it doesn't smell like Mom—it just smells like clean laundry.

Before bed, I stand over my desk and spell:

KANGAROOS ARE QUIET
LOVE ME

Blue

When my eyes open in the morning, the first thing I do is sit up and look at the Scrabble tiles.

KOALAS LOVE TO SLEEP

I wonder if Mom just made that up. I go out to the living room and find Dad's laptop on the coffee table. According to the Web, koalas sleep eighteen to twenty-two hours a day. I lie back on the couch and look up at Sir Ott. "How does she know these things?" I ask him.

First period. Science. I'm walking toward Table Six when Dallas and Carter are suddenly on either side of me.

"You know, Gorgeous, you are really SDP."

Ignore.

"So. Damn. Pathetic." They laugh and walk away.

Ignore.

I slide into my seat. Bob is drawing.

"Why do you do that?" he asks with his head down.

"Do what?"

"Do *nothing.*"

It's like the hard G and the soft G, is what I want to tell Bob. The hard G goes to school, and nothing can hurt him. And the soft G is the one who's talking to you right now. Except he's only talking in my head. I used to know which one was the real me, but now I'm not so sure. Now it's like maybe there is no real me.

Mr. Landau is asking for volunteers. He can't quite hide the surprise in his voice when he sees my arm up, and he calls me to the front. I'm surprised too, actually.

The next thing I know, I'm sitting on a chair at the front of the room with my mouth open and a white paper reinforcement perched like a bull's-eye on the tip of my tongue. Mr. Landau dips a Q-tip into some blue water that he assures me is nontoxic and swabs my tongue with it. Then he gets out his digital camera, takes a close-up, and *projects* the picture onto the whiteboard, explaining to the class that we are looking at the blue tongue-flesh protruding through the hole in the reinforcement that is still in my mouth, magnified ten thousand times.

"Oh—Georges," Mr. Landau says. "You can spit that out now."

I stagger back to Table Six, where Bob English Who Draws is looking pretty sorry for me. He doodles something in his notebook and shoves it over: Above a mean-looking elf he's drawn a thought bubble that says:

That sux. Y did yu raze yer hand?

"You're the one who told me to *do* something," I whisper.

1 1 1

He takes back his paper, scribbles, shoves it back over to me.

I ment abowt DALLAS, yu dork!

I knew that, of course. I still have no idea why I raised my hand. Just to stop myself from thinking so much, maybe.

Everyone stares at the gross blue bumps on my tongue. Mr. Landau is yelling over the retching noises.

"You all have tongues that look like this!" he shouts. "Those are the fungiform papillae!"

"It's a *fungus?*" Carter shrieks over the gagging.

"No!" Mr. Landau says. "The papillae house the taste buds. Let's count them!" But it's useless.

"Silence!" Mr. Landau booms.

Everyone shuts up.

Mr. Landau explains that not everyone has the same number of taste buds. Some people have more, and they're called supertasters, and some have an average number, and they are regular, and some have less. They're called nontasters. He has painted my tongue blue so that we can easily count the number of whitish taste buds inside the circle of the reinforcement. The average number is thirty.

He counts out loud, and it turns out that I'm short a few taste buds. I have twenty-six. I am officially below average. Thank you, Mr. Landau.

"Now we know why Gorgeous loves school lunch!" Carter Dixon says in the cafeteria. "He can't taste it!" He bumps his tray into my ribs.

"He probably eats dog food for dinner!" Dallas Llewellyn says, mouth wide open and full of chewed bagel. "The taste test is coming up, G. You know what I call it? The G-test. You know why? Because it's going to tell us what we already know—that you're not normal. You're the biggest geek-sack in the seventh grade. You're like a big phlegmy wad of geek, Gorgeous. Do you know that about yourself?"

Mandy frowns at her bagel. "That's not really what the taste test is about, Dallas. It's love or death, remember?"

"Not this year," Dallas tells her. "This year it's about who's the biggest steaming pile of spaz."

She looks him in the eye. "Maybe it's not up to you. You ever think of that?"

Dallas wrinkles his nose like he smells something. "Maybe it is up to me. And maybe I say that you're not going to marry Gabe after all. Maybe Gabe actually thinks you're kind of gross. You ever think of *that*?"

Mandy walks away saying, "Blah-blah-blah-whatever!" But her face is all red and I almost feel sorry for her.

Dallas turns to me. "You know what? I bet the taste test is going to prove that you're the only freak in the class. You can't even *taste stuff*. Think about what a colossal freak that makes you."

Lunch is macaroni and cheese, crusty on the top the way I like it.

Last period. Gym. It's Friday again, so Ms. Warner and I do our high five.

The whiteboard says *Capture the Flag!*

Normally I don't mind *Capture the Flag!* because it's pretty easy to fly under the radar: I run around the edges of the game, I get a little exercise, and I don't attempt anything stupid.

But Ms. Warner has decided that today I will be a captain.

"G is captain of the blue team," she announces, and everybody groans. She's just trying to be nice, of course, but I'm disappointed in her. I thought she knew me better than this. Because being a captain is exactly the kind of thing I could never care about.

She looks at me. "C'mon, G. Blue team. Step up."

So I walk up to her, and she smiles.

"Blue *tongue* team," Dallas says, and Mandy laughs. I guess she and Dallas made up.

"And Mandy is the captain of the red team," Ms. Warner says. Mandy claps, jumps up and down, and hugs a few of her friends as if she's just been crowned prom queen in a bad TV movie. She runs up to stand on the other side of Ms. Warner. The rest of the class lines up against the wall.

Now I will have to "pick my team." And I have to be careful, because if a kid is picked last, it can absolutely destroy his or her self-confidence. I decide that the best thing to do is to choose the kids who are normally picked last, *first*. I know exactly who they are. Everyone in the room knows who they are.

Mandy looks more and more confused as I make my way through the smallest, least athletic, most officially uncool kids in the class. Ms. Warner is giving me knowing looks. If we could talk, I would remind her that I never asked to be captain, and that my goals as captain are probably different from most people's. And I'm having fun, I realize.

I let my team members pick code names. Joanna is Spike; Karl and Carl are Smoke and Fire; Bob English Who Draws is Squid; Kevin is Shark Attack; Natasha Khan is Mist; David Rosen is Stingray; Eliza Donan is Laser; Chad, Anita, and Paul are Thing One, Thing Two, and Thing Three; and I am Mask. This eats a couple of minutes. Mandy is complaining to Ms. Warner that we aren't "taking the game seriously," but Ms. Warner doesn't rush us. Everyone on Mandy's team looks competitive and grouchy.

We play. Most of us get our flags pulled and land in jail, and the rest of us plot elaborate rescue missions. Whenever we get a jailbreak, Paul, aka Thing Three, streaks around the gym with both arms up yelling "Blue Team! It's what's for breakfast!" Anita, aka Thing Two, explains that this means Paul is having a good time.

We ignore the red team's flag. We've hidden our flag really well. Karl, aka Smoke, had the idea of tucking it around the basketball hoop. Smoke is tall.

Carter Dixon and Dallas Llewellyn are getting angry. Mandy complains that our flag is nowhere. Ms. Warner assures her that it is somewhere.

"Well, I'm not going through anyone's *pants* or anything," Mandy says. Ms. Warner tells Mandy that our flag is in plain view.

I think of my fortune from Yum Li's: *Why don't you look up once in a while? Is something wrong with your neck?* I'm laughing when the bell goes off. Even though most of my team is incarcerated, it's officially a tie because they never found our flag.

I'm walking out the door when Ms. Warner calls out, "Happy weekend, G. See you on the dark side of Sunday. Get it? The dark side of Sunday? Monday!"

"Hi, G," Carter Dixon says to me at Bennie's after school. I've already made my selection, which is peanut M&M's, otherwise known as one of the world's perfect foods, and I'm waiting for Bennie to take my money and count my change back to me.

"Yeah G, good game today," Dallas Llewellyn says. He drapes an arm over my shoulders.

"G as in *gorgeous*," Carter says.

"G as in *geek*," Dallas says.

"*D* as in *definitely*," Carter says.

"*D* as in *Dallas*," I point out, trying to be helpful. "Soon you guys will know the whole alphabet."

Dallas can move pretty quickly. He has me up against Bennie's potato-chip rack faster than you can say sour cream and onion. I feel the chips against my back, and I'm thinking that a thousand bags of potato chips wouldn't be the worst way to break a fall.￣

"You!" Bennie shouts, pointing two fingers at Carter and Dallas. "Out!" He grabs an open bag of Doritos out of Carter's hand and shakes it in his face. "*Out.*"

Even the high school kids in our neighborhood know better than to mess with Bennie. He learned to fight when he was growing up in Cairo. He says they don't fool around over there.

When Dallas and Carter are gone, Bennie whirls on me. "You're fighting? Since when?"

I shrug.

"I'll tell you something," Bennie says. "That kid, Dallas . . ."

"Yeah?"

"His real name is David."

I laugh. "I know. He changed it in third grade."

Bennie shakes his head. "What's wrong with the name David? Perfectly good name! Seventy-five cents for the M&M's." I give him a dollar, and he counts back my change: "A nickel is *eighty*, a dime is *ninety*, and another dime makes *one dollar*!"

He'll never just hand you a quarter.

At home, there's a note under my door. Yellow paper, folded into fourths:

> **Departed with suitcase, 12:45 p.m.**
> **Report to Uncle ASAP.**

I've barely had time to read it when the phone starts ringing. I pick it up and say, "I'm on my way."

"Um, on your way where?" a voice asks.

"Bob?"

"Yeah."

"Hey. I thought you were someone else."

"I've been thinking."

"About what?" I'm hoping it isn't more creative spelling.

"About the taste test."

"Oh."

"The thing is, no one really knows what you can or can't taste, right? So even if you don't taste something, you can still act like you do. You know what I mean?"

"Yeah, I guess." He means I can pretend. I may be a non-taster, but when Mr. Landau hands out those chemical papers and tells us to put them in our mouths, I can run for water like everyone else. I don't have to be the freak.

"Just in case," Bob says.

Candy answers the door in a dress and her pig slippers.

"Is Safer home?" I ask.

"Safer is always home."

"Don't be a pain, Candy!" Safer's voice, right behind her. "I'm here *babysitting*. Guess who the baby is? Go away, I need to talk to Georges."

"About what?"

"None of your business. Just go back to whatever you were doing, okay?"

"What do you mean 'whatever I was doing'? You left me there watching for the parrots. I fell asleep! And you owe me a dollar. What time is it, anyway?"

"Time for you to go away."

"What about my dollar?"

"Take the dollar! You know where my dog-walking money is! Geesh."

"*Geesh* yourself!" She walks down the hallway.

"What took you so long?" Safer asks, but he doesn't wait for an answer. "Mr. X stayed in his apartment all morning. And then he left with one of the big suitcases. I caught him on the lobbycam."

I don't remind him that I still haven't even *seen* Mr. X, let alone familiarized myself with his luggage.

"You think he went away somewhere? On a trip?"

"Can't say for sure. But it's an opportunity. I'm going back in."

"Back in," I repeat.

"Only first we have to make a list."

"A list," I repeat.

"Yes, Georges, a *list*. Of everything that can possibly be opened with a key."

"What about a desk drawer?" I say, when we're settled in our beanbags. "Or a briefcase?"

"Desk drawer," Safer says, writing in his notebook. "Briefcase."

"Or maybe a cabinet," I say. "Some old cabinets have little keys like that—did you see anything old-looking in his apartment? Once my dad showed me this desk at an antiques store that had a secret drawer, behind this panel—"

Safer looks up and stares at me. "This is an area of strength for you, Georges."

"Not really. I've just been dragged to a lot of antiques stores."

He smiles. "Still. You're thinking like a spy. It's progress."

Which makes me feel good, actually. Like I'm possibly getting better at something.

And then, as if he can read my mind, Safer says, "You're not a novice anymore, Georges. Is *novice* on your famous vocabulary list?"

"I know what *novice* means."

"Good. Then you know what it means to be done with novice work."

I'm not sure I like where this is going. "So what's after novice work?"

Safer gives me his serious look. "Night work."

Break and Enter (#2)

Night work means sleeping with my cell phone stuffed into a tube sock, under my ear. It's on vibrate, and it goes off at two in the morning, dragging me from what feels like the bottom of the ocean.

"This is my third call," Safer says when I fumble it out of the sock. "Now that you aren't a novice, you have to learn to be a lighter sleeper."

"How does a person *learn* that?"

"I'll be outside your door in sixty seconds."

"Now what?" I say when we're standing on my doormat.

"You're not dressed." Safer takes in my T-shirt and pajama bottoms. He's wearing jeans and a button-down oxford, tucked in.

"What's the point? You said the whole idea is that we aren't supposed to see anyone else."

He starts up the stairs. "It's just—spies get *dressed.* You know?"

When we get up to Mr. X's, we both automatically look for the gum wrapper, which is still stuck in the door.

"Told you," Safer says.

"And can you guarantee that he won't come back in the next twenty minutes?"

"In the middle of the night?" Safer steps out of his shoes and lines them up on one side of Mr. X's doormat.

"I don't think I can go in there," I say.

Safer opens one hand, showing me the little gold key. "I have to know what this opens, Georges. And that isn't going to happen if we just stand here whispering in the hallway, is it?"

I shake my head. "I can't. It's not right."

He looks at the ceiling for a second. "I could use your expertise in there, Georges. But if you aren't comfortable with it, you can stand guard."

"Stand here, you mean? In my pajamas? What if someone walks by?"

He pulls his credit card out of his back pocket. "The pajamas were your idea."

"Like it would make a lot of sense for me to be standing here in a James Bond suit!"

"*Shhh.* No one is going to walk by, Georges. It's two in the morning."

"Then why do you need a lookout?"

He shoves the credit card between the door and the frame, just above the knob. "Look, I need to know. Do I have a lookout or not?"

"No," I say. "You don't."

"Fine." Safer forces the credit card down in one quick

motion and turns the doorknob at the same time. The door opens, and he slips inside, closing it silently behind him.

I pace back and forth in the hall for a minute and then run back downstairs. I get into bed and lie still, but sleep is not happening. I listen for footsteps above me, though the fact is that I have never heard a single sound from Mr. X's apartment.

That's when my cell phone goes off. I've left it on my desk, where it buzzes against the wood and makes my heart practically explode.

"Hello?"

"If you were a key, what would you open?"

"Safer," I whisper, "where are you?"

"You know exactly where I am, Georges. In fact, you're the only person who does."

"Oh my God—whose phone are you on? Are you calling me from *his* phone?"

"It's not long-distance. He'll never know."

"Safer!"

"The key, Georges. Think."

"Get *out* of there. You're freaking me out!"

"Uh-oh," Safer says.

"Uh-oh *what*?"

"Shhh—hold on."

I hold on. I'm squeezing my phone so hard I'm surprised it doesn't shoot out of my hand and hit the ceiling. "Safer?" I whisper. "Are you okay?"

"Wait," he says, "I—" And then he hangs up.

Or someone hangs up for him.

* * *

Before I can even think, I'm back on Mr. X's doormat, staring at Safer's loafers. I put my ear to the door—nothing. I hold my breath, put my hand on the doorknob, and turn. The door is unlocked.

Quietly, quietly, I swing it open and step into Mr. X's apartment.

It's pretty dark in there, so I can't see much—a wicker table piled with mail and magazines, an old-fashioned umbrella stand, and a green plastic watering can on the floor. I can see one corner of the kitchen because the light is on in there. It looks just like ours, with a big white fridge and white counters.

"Safer?" I whisper.

Safer saunters out of the kitchen, sipping a bottle of water. "If you were a key," he says, "what would you open?"

I'm speechless mad. I grab Safer's arm and pull him into the hallway. He lets me.

"What's wrong with you?" I say when the door has closed.

Safer steps into his loafers. "Nothing is wrong. Well, there is one thing—I couldn't find anything I could open with this." He holds the key up between two fingers.

"You scared me to death. And you—you turned me into a criminal! Do you realize that?"

"A *criminal*? You're a hero!"

"What are you talking about?"

"You came to save me, didn't you? That's hero behavior."

"I don't care. I walked into someone's apartment. In the middle of the night. That's breaking and entering!"

"It's not like you took anything," Safer says. "Thirsty?" He holds the water bottle out to me.

"Did you steal that? Did you open his *refrigerator?*"

"I was parched."

"You're crazy." I start down the stairs.

"I gave you a gift," Safer calls after me softly. "Now you know exactly what kind of person you are. You're brave, Georges! Your skills need work, but you're brave!"

Heat

Saturday morning, Dad wants us to go to MoMA, which is the Museum of Modern Art, which is "just across town" from Mom's hospital, where he says we can "pop in" for lunch.

I tell him that hospital food is not my idea of lunch, and besides, I have a lot of homework. Dad settles for breakfast together at Everybody's Favorite Diner and then I walk him to the subway. He's got Mom's robe and some of those yogurts she likes in a plastic bag.

When I get back to our lobby, I don't feel like going home. I don't want to chill with Sir Ott, I don't want to eat string cheese, I don't want to watch TV, and I definitely don't want to do homework. So I buzz Safer, even though it's on the early side and I'm officially still annoyed at him for acting like a lunatic last night. He answers immediately.

"Did you buy any *gum* while you were out?" Safer asks through the intercom. "I'm really in the mood for *gum*."

"I'm still mad at you," I tell him.

"I'm all *out* of *gum*. I had some *gum* this morning, but now I'm *out*. So hurry up."

Safer must think I'm stupid or something. He buzzes me in, and I head for the stairs. On four, I glance at Mr. X's door and see the gum wrapper tucked neatly into the doorframe. Safer must have put it back last night after I stomped off.

But I'm not up to spying today. I pluck the wrapper out with two fingers and run up to Safer's. I ring the bell and stand there holding the gum wrapper out in front of me, totally forgetting that Safer never answers the door.

"What's that for?" Candy says when she sees me holding out the gum wrapper.

"Nothing," I say quickly. "People are slobs!"

"That's true," she says, looking at me funny.

I change the subject. "You never told me how old you are. Is it a big secret or something?"

She narrows her eyes. "You never asked. I'm ten."

"Ten," I repeat.

"Almost ten. I'm small for my age."

"Yeah."

"If I was in school, I'd be in fourth grade. I looked it up."

"Yeah, that sounds right."

"If I went to your school," she asks me, "would I be the smallest fourth grader?"

"I don't know the fourth grade that well," I tell her. "But there's actually one kid in *my* grade who's about your size."

"Really? Who?"

"Teresa Conchetti. She's always been super-short."

"Oh."

That came out wrong. "But she's really smart, and also funny. She sits at the cool table and everything." I don't add that, last I knew, Jason had a crush on Teresa Conchetti, and that he actually stood up for her once in sixth grade when Dallas was calling her Terry Conchesty. But that was before.

"With you, you mean?"

"What?"

"She sits at the cool table—with you?"

"I don't sit at the cool table," I tell her. "I wouldn't even want to sit there."

"Why not?"

"Because half the kids at that table are total jerks."

She looks at me. "Then why do the other half of them sit there?"

I've wondered this too. Specifically, I've wondered it about Jason. "I don't know. Maybe they think that if they sit there, they won't be victims, or whatever."

"So why don't you sit there?"

"Because I would rather be a jerk's victim than a jerk's friend."

She nods. "The friend of my enemy is my enemy. Somebody said that once. So maybe the friend of a jerk is a jerk."

I look at her. "Maybe."

"You guys are both forgetting the most important rule," a voice behind us says.

"Oh, yeah?" Candy turns and looks Safer up and down. "What's the most important rule?"

"'Keep your friends close, but keep your enemies closer.'"

"Meaning what, exactly?" Candy asks.

"Meaning maybe the friends of the jerks are only pretending to be their friends. Maybe they recognize the enemy and they're keeping him close."

No wonder these two don't go to school. They would take it all a little too seriously.

"You know what I would do?" Candy says. "I would decide that my table is the cool table. Anyone could sit there. And that would be that."

"You can't just do that," I tell her.

"Why not? Why do you get to make the rules?"

"*Me?* Trust me. I have nothing to do with making the rules."

"Weren't you the one who just told me I couldn't sit at the cool table?"

"I didn't say that!"

"You did, Georges. Think about it."

"*Goodbye,* Candy," Safer says. "Georges and I have things to do."

Candy humphs and disappears into the kitchen, and I'm not all that sorry to see her go.

When I'm alone with Safer, I show him the gum wrapper. "Looks like Mr. X came home," I say. "I guess it was a short trip."

He looks surprised. Very surprised. He takes the wrapper and rolls it slowly between his fingers. "It was on the doormat?"

"Yeah. Bummer, right? Now you can't act like a crazy person. I guess your whole day is shot."

"Frustrating." Safer stares hard at the gum wrapper. Then he looks me in the eyes, and I get the distinct feeling that he knows I'm lying. Then he holds out his flask. "Coffee?"

"Hey, did you tell him yet?" Candy calls from the kitchen. "You told me not to tell him, and then you didn't even tell him!"

Safer drops his arm. "The parrots are back."

"The parrots are back!" Candy says.

We take turns looking at them through the binoculars. One of them—I can't tell, but Safer says it's always the same one—keeps leaving and then flying back to the nest.

"He's carrying twigs," Safer says. "Rebuilding."

"Aren't there two of them? How come the other one doesn't help?"

"I wonder if she's getting ready to lay eggs," he says, flipping through his notebook. "It's about that time, I think."

We can't talk about Mr. X because Candy is there, but for once Safer doesn't tell her to go away. She brings out her stash and we have a little welcome-back party for the parrots: Starbursts and the last of the Chicks, Ducks, and Bunnies SweeTarts.

Pigeon wanders out of his room right before lunch, looking sleepy. Safer tells him about the parrots being back, and they high-five.

"How goes it, Georges?" Pigeon asks me.

"It goes okay."

"You taking care of our boy?" He palms Safer's head.

"I guess," I say, thinking that Safer pretty much takes care of himself.

Pigeon smiles at me. "Good."

* * *

Safer's mom is at an all-day wedding and Saturday is his dad's busiest day at driving school, so Safer makes scrambled eggs for lunch and keeps his promise to teach me how.

"The secret of good scrambled eggs," he tells me, "is very low heat." He turns the flame way down and stands there stirring the eggs in the pan forever, but when they finally cook, they're delicious. Candy makes toast and provides dessert.

Then we just hang out doing nothing, which is exactly what I feel like doing. Dad calls my cell to check on me and puts me on the phone with Mom and she doesn't sound too tired.

When it's almost dinnertime, I tell Safer I have to meet my dad downstairs.

"We're going to Yum Li's again. You want to come with us?"

"I can't," Safer says. "Dad's taking Pigeon to his track meet, and my mom has the wedding. I have to stay home with Candy."

"You could both come," I say. "My dad won't mind."

"I love Yum Li's!" Candy says.

"No," Safer says. "Mom left us ziti."

"Isn't that the ziti Pigeon made?" Candy makes a face. "His ziti is terrible. I want to go to Yum Li's."

"No," Safer says.

"*Yes,*" Candy says.

"*No,*" Safer says.

Candy walks up close to Safer and growls right in his

face—or up toward his face, I guess, since she's a head shorter than he is: "I *hate* you."

Safer doesn't say anything. He just takes a step back.

She stomps down the hall and into her room, slamming the door so hard the windows shake.

Safer looks at me.

"Um," I say, "maybe another time?"

He smiles. "She has a temper."

He walks me to the door, and I tell him I officially forgive him for what he pulled last night. Safer says, "Yeah, I forgive you too," and he puts a fresh gum wrapper into my hand.

He knows I lied, but I have no idea how he knows.

A Message from the Chef

We can't see the parrots from our apartment, but when I'm walking to Yum Li's with Dad, I realize that I can see the nest a little bit from the street. I tell Dad about how the birds' grandparents escaped from Kennedy Airport, and I point at the air conditioner they live under.

It's that time of day when the sun seems to come closer and closer, sending this incredible light almost sideways, and all of a sudden we see a flash of color and then, for one long second, a bright green fan of feathers against the sky.

"Wow!" Dad says. "That's amazing." And I can tell he's not faking it for my sake.

When we walk into the restaurant, Yum Li is standing next to the coatrack in his cooking clothes, which Dad calls his chef whites.

"You again?" Yum Li says when he sees us. "Did you forget where the grocery store is or something? I'll draw you a map."

Dad laughs and starts to walk toward an open table, but I don't move because I'm stuck in the spot I was standing on when I realized that the big table in the middle of the room is full of Jason's family. And Jason. And Carter Dixon.

Now Dad has seen them. He booms "Hello!" and starts chatting away with Jason's parents.

"How's Sara doing?" I hear Jason's mom ask.

I force myself to move. I don't get why I'm feeling so upset. I see Jason and Carter practically all day, every day.

I walk over to their table, and I smile while Jason's parents tell me I got tall. Jason waves and says hi. Carter Dixon is looking at his plate. I follow Dad to our corner.

"You know what? We should have some people over soon," Dad says. "When things calm down."

I nod. "The chicken or the beef?" I ask him. Because we always get one or the other. Like it isn't enough that we come to the same place over and over. We also have to eat the same thing.

"Whatever you want," he says.

When we've eaten and finished our oranges, our waitress sets down the cookie plate. "Three fortunes," she says, "plus a special message from the chef."

Yum Li has put the third fortune cookie into the smallest to-go container I have ever seen. And underneath it is a napkin with writing on it.

Dad picks up the napkin, turns it back and forth, and laughs. "Not bad!"

It's a hand-drawn map, with a big red X on the corner where the nearest Met Foods is—the same one where that bird flew into the glass.

Directions to the grocery store.

* * *

When we walk into the apartment, we hear a voice leaving a message on the answering machine: "It's Sophia here, Martin. I'm just checking in to—"

Dad grabs the phone and walks to his bedroom. "Hello? I'm here, I'm here. What's—" The door closes behind him.

I leave the tiny white box from Yum Li's next to the Scrabble tiles on my desk and spell out a note for Mom:

GOOD NIGHT COOKIE
LOVE ME

Then I fall asleep faster than I think I have ever fallen asleep in my life.

Break and Enter (#3)

Sunday morning, the phone rings and stops, rings and stops, slowly tugging me out of sleep until I'm awake enough to wonder why Dad isn't answering it.

I sit up and look at my desk. The white box from Yum Li's is gone, and there's a message from Mom:

YUM COOKIE
LOVE YOU

The phone starts up again.

"Today's the day, Georges. Mr. X went out this morning. We're going to find whatever the key opens. This is it."

"No," I say. "There's no way either of us is going back into that apartment."

"Last time, Georges. I promise. Scout's honor."

"*No.*"

"Have I ever asked you for anything?" Safer says.

I walk to the fridge, where Dad has left a note that says @ *the hospital*.

"Are you kidding?" I ask Safer. "You asked me to be your lookout the other night while you *committed a crime*."

"You said no," he points out.

"And then you tricked me into going into a stranger's apartment."

"That was purely voluntary. Very brave. Anyway, you said you forgave me."

"You asked me to stall your mom when you were going through Mr. X's laundry. I looked like an idiot and got brown goop on my leg."

"Besides that."

You asked me to lie to my dad, I think.

"Well, I'm asking for something now," he says, as if we've just established that he's a saint who's never asked a single person for anything. "I need you to back me up on the lobbycam. That's all, Georges. It's hardly anything."

"And I'm saying *no*."

"This is the last time, Georges. I'm going to hang up and give you a few minutes to think about it."

I eat a bowl of cereal.

The phone rings.

"The answer is still no," I say.

"Don't you ever say hello?" It's Bob English Who Draws.

"Sorry! I thought you were—"

"Someone else. I know."

"What's up?"

"I've been thinking."

"Again?"

"Very funny. Look, I figure the taste test will probably be Tuesday or Wednesday. The unit is almost over."

He's right. In two or three days, I'll officially be the biggest steaming pile of spaz in the seventh grade.

"So if you're absent on Tuesday and Wednesday, you'll almost definitely miss it."

"You mean skip class?"

"Of course not. I'm just saying if you're not feeling well or something."

"I feel fine."

"Think about it."

I tell Bob I'll think about it. As soon as I put the phone down, it rings again.

"I know what I'm looking for this time," Safer says. "But I would feel a lot better if you had my back. I'll give you some more time to think about it."

I get dressed, telling myself I won't answer the phone when he calls. But then I do.

"Do you have my back, Georges? Can I count on you?"

I stand there holding the phone. What I'm thinking is that Safer is the only actual friend I've got, unless you count Bob English Who Draws. Should I count Bob English Who Draws?

"You still there?" Safer asks.

"I'm here." I walk over to the lobbycam. Standing in my own private hallway looking at my own private intercom can't be against the law, can it?

"Fine," I tell him. "But this is the last time. The lobby is all clear. You're good to go."

"I knew it, Georges! Knew I could count on you. Look— forget banging on the pipe. I'm on Pigeon's cell phone, so I'll bring it with me and we can keep talking. If you see Mr. X on the lobbycam, just give me a shout."

Great. Burglary by telephone. I'm probably about to take one giant step toward the definition of conspiracy.

I hear a *swish-swish* sound through the phone and I know Safer is on the move—it's the same sound I hear when Dad sticks his cell phone in his pocket and it accidentally calls home.

Swish-swish.

Swish-swish.

Then nothing for a little while.

Then Safer's voice: "Okay, I'm in."

"So what are you looking for, exactly?"

"A book," he says.

"A book that locks?"

"Yes—I did some research online. I think it's a key to a diary—something old. He must lock it for a reason. Maybe he keeps a list of his victims or something."

"Just make sure you don't end up on that list."

"Why are you whispering, Georges?"

"Because this is crazy!" I say. "It's the middle of the day. What if he comes home and walks in on you?"

"Now you're whispering and yelling at the same time. Who knew you were so talented? Anyway, that's what you're there for, Georges. To protect me."

Which makes me feel vaguely sick.

"Okay," Safer says. "There are a couple of bookshelves, and then I have to go through the desk drawers and stuff. I'm sticking the phone in my pocket, but I'll leave it on so you can hear me."

My mouth is dry, but I don't want to risk the thirty seconds it would take to get water from the kitchen sink. *Think of Safer*, I tell myself. *He's crazy, but he's your friend. And he's up there with the handsaw, alone.*

"Okay, the bookshelves have just regular books," I hear him say. "I'm checking the desk drawers."

Swish-swish.

"Nothing in the desk drawers. I'm going to check over by his bed."

Swish-swish.

Swish-swish.

The intercom turns itself off, and I push the button to reactivate it. When the picture comes back, there's someone in the lobby. A tall man in a black jacket, with a suitcase.

"Safer," I whisper.

Nothing. Not even a *swish-swish.*

I realize I'm whispering into Safer's pocket.

"Safer!" I yell.

Nothing.

The tall man has let himself into the lobby. I start pushing random buttons on my phone, thinking it might make Safer's phone beep and catch his attention. The tall man is waiting for the elevator.

I run to the kitchen and grab a big spoon. I start banging on the heating pipe, three quick, three slow, three quick. I drop the spoon and push more phone buttons. "Safer, Safer!" I yell.

I hear a dial tone. I must have disconnected the call by

pushing so many buttons. Stupid. So stupid! I don't even know Pigeon's cell phone number, so I can't call him back.

On the lobbycam, the tall man is getting into the elevator, dragging his suitcase behind him. I give up on the phone and run out our front door, into the hallway. I take a deep breath and push the elevator button. I can't let Mr. X find Safer in his apartment. I have to stall him. And if I'm there, the guy can't kill him, because there'll be a witness.

Unless he kills both of us.

The elevator is coming. *Maybe it isn't Mr. X,* I think. *Maybe this is someone completely different, here to stay with a friend. Maybe it's some French person visiting Mr. Gervais on the fifth floor.* I breathe.

The elevator door opens. The tall man is standing there in his black jacket next to his suitcase. I notice his pants are black too. Lots of people wear black, I remind myself. Probably French people, especially.

The man smiles at me. "Going up?"

No trace of an accent.

Mr. X

I nod. But I don't get in.

"Well, come aboard, son! I've had a long trip, and I am ready to be home."

I step into the elevator.

"Where to?" he says. His hand is hovering in front of the buttons.

Wait a minute. This can't be Mr. X. Mr. X *doesn't talk.* Relief rushes at me. I exhale.

"Uh—four," I croak.

"Four! Same as me."

Unless Safer was wrong about Mr. X not talking.

"Well, me and the Koffers. But you must know that, if that's where you're headed. I thought they were away until June. Maybe their trip was cut short too."

I try to think like a spy. "Oh yeah, they're away. I'm feeding their cat."

"Cat?" He looks confused. "Since when do the Koffers have a cat?"

"I mean, *plants*. I'm feeding their plants. I fed somebody's cat last week."

We get to four. It doesn't take long for the elevator to go exactly one floor up. He holds the door open for me. "So you're a businessman, huh? Maybe you could feed my dog sometime. I've got a dog walker already, but I could probably find some work for you." He smiles. He kind of reminds me of a friendly fisherman from a commercial for frozen fish sticks.

"You have a dog?" I ask stupidly.

"Yup. She's been away, though, like me. I get a lot of travel this time of year, so I lent her to my cousin out on Long Island. His kids are crazy about her."

Something is off. I realize that something is off, but mainly I'm worried about Safer. I can't let this man walk in and find Safer going through his stuff.

I'm standing there without any idea what to do next. What do you do to distract a potential killer who seems like one of the nicest guys in the world? I remind myself that in movies the bad guys are always pretending to be good guys. That way when they suddenly act evil, it's extra-scary. Extra-scary makes good movies. But I have no desire to experience it in real life.

He's getting his keys out. I stand in front of the Koffers' door. Whoever they are.

He's watching me. "Everything okay over there?" He's got his door open and he's pushing his suitcase in ahead of him. I'm imagining Safer somewhere inside, having the realization that Mr. X has come home. That he's trapped in there.

"Um, no," I say. "I—forgot the key. I'll have to go home

and get it." I'm listening hard for Safer. What is he thinking right now? Will he come running out of the apartment? Will he hide under the bed? Whatever he's doing, I figure I must be buying him some time, at least.

"Oh, don't bother," Mr. X says. "I have a set of their keys inside. Wait right here."

"No," I call after him, "it's okay. Anyway, I have this, um, plant food downstairs. Special plant food. I forgot that, too."

He smiles. "Plant food? Is this for that little spider plant they have in the kitchen? I never realized they were so serious about that thing."

"Um, it's sick. It's got a disease. I have the medicine and stuff. For it."

"Oh." Now he's just staring at me, and it's obvious he thinks I'm weird, like he's not so sure he wants me feeding his dog after all.

Safer's had plenty of time to hide by now. He hasn't made a run for the door, so I figure he must be planning to wait until Mr. X goes into the bathroom or something, and then he'll come out from under the bed and make his escape. I might as well let him get on with it.

"So, bye!" I say.

And I run back downstairs.

The phone is ringing when I fling my door open. I'm sweating and my head is pounding.

"Hello?"

"Hey, we must have gotten cut off." It's Safer. "You still on the cam?"

"Safer, are you okay? Where are you?"

"At you-know-who's. I'm right by the front door, ready to leave. Just checking in for the all-clear."

"For the all clear? Safer, are you still—upstairs? At Mr. X's?"

"Yup, ready to go when you say when. You won't believe what I found, Georges. I have a lot to tell you."

And that's when I figure it out.

It's like Sir Ott—all those little dots coming together to make a picture.

"Just a second, Safer. I think one of the Koffers is coming in. You better sit tight for a minute."

"Really? Okay. I'll wait for your word."

"Don't move." I put the phone receiver down very gently on the kitchen counter, and then I run up to Safer's apartment.

I don't ring the bell. I knock, very quietly.

Candy answers the door. "What's wrong with the bell?"

"Nothing. Is Safer here?"

"Of course," she says. "Safer is always here." And she lets the door swing open. I rush past her and down the hall to the living room. Quietly.

His back is to me. He's standing at the window in his socks, holding Pigeon's cell phone up to his ear with one hand. In his other hand are the binoculars. He's looking through the window. At the parrots.

"Georges?" I hear him say into the phone, "I'm ready to make my move. All clear?"

"All clear," I say loudly. "Make your move, Safer."

Safer spins around. There's a look on his face that I've never seen before.

"You're a liar," I say. "You lied about everything."

Safer says nothing, just keeps giving me that look and standing there with the binoculars in one hand and Pigeon's cell phone in the other.

"You never left your apartment," I say. "You never went anywhere."

"I *couldn't* go anywhere this time," Safer says. "Mom asked me to babysit."

"There is no Mr. X. He's just some guy whose dog you walk, right? He's been away this whole week. You've been lying to me since the day I met you. What was the point, Safer? Just your sick sense of humor? Was it that much fun to watch me get all worked up about nothing?"

He shakes his head. "Of course not. It was a game, Georges."

"I'm sick of games! I'm so, so sick of games, and all the stupid—"

"Why are you so upset? This is what friends *do*, Georges."

"Friends? You tricked me. That's what friends do? You give me the creeps, you know that?"

Safer doesn't say anything. What he does is turn back to the window and hold up his binoculars.

"I'm getting out of here," I say. And I stomp down the hallway.

Candy sticks her head out of her room. "What's going on?"

I slam their front door.

Rules of the Game

I call Dad on his cell.

"Just leaving," he says. "Want to meet somewhere for lunch?"

I tell him I'll cook.

He makes me promise no actual flames until he gets home. I spend half an hour shredding up string-cheese sticks and cracking eggs. I peel two cucumbers, cut them up, and put them in a bowl. I stack four pieces of bread next to the toaster.

Dad comes in while I'm setting the table. I make us scrambled eggs with cheese, making sure the cheese is nice and melted before I turn off the heat.

"Can I help?" Dad asks.

"You could salt the cucumbers," I tell him. "And put ice in our glasses."

We eat. "I love scrambled eggs!" Dad announces. "How could I have forgotten how much I love scrambled eggs?"

I sit there thinking the secret to good scrambled eggs was probably the one true thing Safer ever told me.

"So?" Dad says. "Tell me things!"

I pour my heart out. I tell him everything about what happened with Safer and Mr. X, all of it.

"I can't be friends with someone like that," I tell Dad.

"Someone like what?"

"Someone who lies."

"Was it a lie? Or was it a game?"

"I hate games. I hate people who *play* games."

Dad nods. "Maybe you're right to be mad. But isn't playing games a way of being friends?"

"Not if you don't know it's a game!"

"What if he didn't know you didn't know?"

"He knew."

"Maybe he did. Maybe he didn't."

"He did."

"How did all this get started?"

I think. "The Spy Club."

"And did you go down there thinking you would find real spies?"

"No. Obviously."

"So weren't you kind of on notice from the beginning that it was a game?"

"He acted serious. Like he believed it."

"Some games are played that way."

"I hate games," I say.

And then I pour my heart out for the second time in ten minutes, this time about Dallas Llewellyn and Carter Dixon. And the taste test.

Dad looks miserable. "Why didn't you tell me? I could have *done* something, a long time ago."

I shrug. "It's just dumb stuff. You know, kids being kids. I know none of it will matter in a few years."

He stares at me. "Who told you that?"

"Mom. She always says to look at the big picture. How all of the little things don't matter in the long run."

He blinks. "But they matter *now*, Georges. They matter a *lot*. What were you planning to do, just hold your breath all the way through middle school?"

"No. No one can hold their breath that long."

"Look, I know Mom talks about the big picture. She wants you to remember that you'll find new friends, that life is always changing, sometimes in really good ways. But life is also what's happening *now*, Georges. What Dallas and Carter are doing is happening *now*, and you can't just wait for it to be over. We have to do something about it. *Now*."

It's weird, because I know Mom is right about the big picture. But Dad is right too: Life is really just a bunch of *nows*, one after the other.

The dots matter.

"First thing in the morning," Dad says, "I'm going down to school with you and we're airing this whole thing out. There are rules about this kind of thing, Georges. Important ones."

And I feel so good when he says that. I'm about to say yes, let's go to Everybody's Favorite Diner and get egg sandwiches and then walk to school together and all this can be over. But then I hear myself telling him no. Because I have an idea.

There are all kinds of rules. There are written-down school rules like Dad is talking about, and there are rules we just live with without even asking ourselves why. Candy is right. Why shouldn't her table be the cool table? Who says I have to try to steal the other team's flag? Why does Bob have to spell *dumb* with a B?

What if you decided to make your own rules?

"But you'll tell me if you need me?" Dad says after I explain. "Promise me."

"I promise."

"I'm so sorry, Georges. I should have been around more lately. I should have . . . been here, *cooked* for you," he says. "Yum Li is right. It hasn't been easy because Mom hasn't wanted to force you to—"

I stop him. "So cook something," I say.

He looks at me a second, then stands up and starts going through the fridge. "I know," he says. "I know exactly what to cook."

Dad cooks milk shakes. In the blender. Then we kick back with Sir Ott for some baseball. I don't think about Safer, and I don't think about Dallas, or the taste test, or my big idea that may or may not work. I just drink my milk shake, sit next to Dad, and think about how this *now* is the best one I've had in a while.

Before bed that night, I spell Mom a note:

MISS U MIS U MIS U

There's a shortage of S's and only two M's, so the last one is an upside-down W. I fall asleep to the sound of Dad murmuring into the phone behind his bedroom door.

In the morning there's a message from Mom:

ME TOO PICKLE

Blu Teem

"I've been thinking," I tell Bob English on Monday morning.

"Yeah? About what?"

"About the taste test. About the rules."

He leans his head on his hand. "Which ones?"

"All of them." And I tell him my plan.

"I like it," he says. "I like it a lot." He reaches for his bag of Sharpies, fishes around in it, and pulls out a blue one. "Give me your hand."

The former members of the Blue Team are scattered all over the cafeteria at lunchtime—twelve bodies orbiting the white-hot sun of the cool table. There are a few loners like me and Bob, a few twos like Carl and Karl, and one group of three: Chad, Anita, and Paul. We're like Seurat's orange dots hidden in the bright green grass, the ones you don't even see unless you know to look for them.

We talk to half of them at lunch and catch the other five after gym. I explain my plan while Bob stands behind me and flips his blue Sharpie. They all listen carefully and agree right away, but I make each person stop for a second, and I ask, "Are you sure?"

And every one of them says yes, and then holds out one hand, to Bob.

After school, Bob walks me to Bennie's, flipping his Sharpie into the air and catching it. His eyes never leave his blue pen. He doesn't even look for cars at the corner.

"You should really look for cars," I tell him.

"We're a team now," he says. "You were looking for both of us." And then he waves and walks off.

Dad is home when I walk in, sitting on the couch with his laptop. The apartment smells like chicken and garlic.

Safer doesn't call.

There's no note under the door.

I check under my pillow before bed. Nothing.

Taste Test

When we file into the science room on Tuesday, Mr. Landau is leaning back against his desk with his arms crossed.

"PROP," he starts, "is a chemical compound that ten to twenty percent of the human population can't—"

Someone squeals in excitement. There's no other word for it. It's a squeal.

Mr. Landau glares. "—can't taste at all. The other eighty to ninety percent of us can taste PROP. Some will be more sensitive to it than others. It isn't a pleasant taste. Very bitter, in fact."

"Taste-*test*. Taste-*test*," someone starts chanting. It's Carter.

"G-*test*, G-*test*," Dallas says, pointing at me.

Mr. Landau's eyes follow Dallas's finger right to the middle of my chest, and he growls, "One more sound and you're both out of here." I wonder if he even knows what "G-test" stands for, or that his class is now just another way for Dallas to pick his next victim. Or, even better, an excuse to keep picking on me.

Mr. Landau starts talking about chemical compounds and genetic differences, and everyone is bouncing in their seats.

Bob English is messing with his bag of Sharpies. He huddles over his notebook. And then he tears off a sheet of paper, folds it once, and slides it over to me. "Just a reminder," he whispers. "Pass it on."

I open the note and read:

> Reemembur: Blu Teem stiks togethur.
> Smial no madder whut.
> No wadder.

I refold the paper, locate the nearest Blue Team member, who is Natasha Khan at Table Five, and I pass it to her. As she reaches for it, I get a glimpse of the blue dot on her palm.

I watch Natasha read it. Her expression doesn't change. She passes it to Eliza Donan.

Mr. Landau holds up a skinny roll of paper. It looks like a roll of white ribbon. He walks around the room, tearing off strips of paper and handing them out. Mandy stares at hers like it holds the secret of the universe.

Meanwhile, Bob's note is making its way around the room.

Eliza to Kevin.

Kevin to Anita.

Anita to Chad.

Palm to palm.

Dot to dot.

Mr. Landau gets to our table, tears off two slips of magic paper, and hands one to Bob English. Then he hands me mine. It reminds me of a fortune from Yum Li's. A blank one.

"Do you think everyone saw the note?" I ask Bob.

"Think so," he says, tapping his pen cap against his teeth.

"All right," Mr. Landau says finally. "There are twenty-four students in the class. Statistically, at least two of you should not be able to taste the compound on the paper."

I can see Mandy's hands shaking.

"When I give you the signal, place the strips of paper on your tongues," Mr. Landau says. "If you do taste the compound, it will be strong and unpleasantly bitter, so you may line up—*calmly, please*—at the fountain for water."

I see Dallas's mouth moving—I realize he's mouthing "G-test, G-test," staying silent so that Mr. Landau doesn't kick him out. Carter is rocking in his seat, keeping time with Dallas.

I look over at Jason, but he's paying no attention to them. I see him tap the hand of David Rosen, the last Blue Team member to read Bob's note. David glances at Bob, who shrugs and looks at me.

Who is Jason now, I wonder? If he reads that note and passes it to Dallas or Carter, everything will be ruined.

I nod, and David slides the note over to Jason. I watch him read it, and wonder if he knows about Ben Franklin's spelling reform movement. I doubt it.

"All right," Mr. Landau says. "Let's get this over with."

When I put my paper on my tongue, a bitter taste fills my mouth and nose. It turns out that I am a PROP taster, like 80 or 90 percent of the world. And what I'm tasting right now is pretty awful.

But I pretend otherwise. I take a deep breath, smile, and look around the room. Bob English is next to me, doing the same. I can see his eyes watering.

Mandy is screeching and running for the water fountain, waving both hands in front of her mouth. She looks accusingly at Gabe, who's just sitting there looking surprised that nothing has happened. His eyes aren't watering. He really doesn't taste it.

A few kids are already lined up in front of Mandy for water—Dallas and Carter are there, of course.

Natasha Khan stays in her seat.

Eliza Donan.

Carl and Karl.

David Rosen.

Chad Levine.

Paul Kim.

Anita Wu.

Joanna Washington.

Kevin Anderson.

All in their seats. All smiling.

Jason is still in his seat, too. He gives David Rosen a thumbs-up.

And then it is over. The taste in my mouth starts to go away. Jason, Gabe, Teresa Conchetti, and every member of the Blue Team are still in their seats.

"Fifteen nontasters," Mr. Landau says. "Not at all what I expected. What an interesting group of people you have turned out to be."

Dallas lifts his head from the water fountain and looks at the fifteen kids sitting in their seats. I can see his eyes bouncing from me to Jason to Teresa to Gabe to everyone else. He wipes his mouth and mutters one word: "Idiotic."

At lunch, Dallas and Carter and Jason sit together with Teresa, Mandy, Gabe, and the others. They all have bagels. Nothing has changed, but I feel different.

I eat my lasagna and do my homework. Bob English draws next to me, eating a sandwich from home. We don't talk much, but it's nice to have him there. I'm about to get up to dump my tray when Bob looks up and barks out a laugh.

"What?"

"You know what that was? This morning? Sitting there smiling with that gross taste in my mouth? Watching Dallas's lamosity get totally frustrated?"

Lamosity is not technically a word. But who am I to say that Bob shouldn't use it?

"No," I say. "What was it?"

"It was sweet. And it was bitter. Get it?" He raises his eyebrows. "It was *bittersweet*."

Which cracks us up.

Chad, Anita, and Paul are coming toward us.

"Hey, Chad needs his dot touched up," Anita tells Bob. "His got partly rubbed off." Chad opens his hand to reveal a blue smudge.

"Touched up?" Bob asks. "What for?"

"We're *keeping* them, aren't we?" She puts one hand on her hip. "Isn't that the point? That we're all like—whatever? A team?"

"Yeah," I say, while Bob finds his blue Sharpie. "That's exactly what it means."

"Blue Team!" Paul says. "It's what's for breakfast!"

We all watch Bob fill in Chad's blue dot, and I know that something has changed after all.

Knock, Knock

When I get to our building, Safer is sitting cross-legged in one of the lobby chairs, reading a book. He doesn't look up when I come in, so I pretend not to see him. I go over to the elevator and push the button.

"Hi," I hear him say.

I turn around. "Hey."

"I was thinking—I never did tell you."

"Tell me what?"

"About my name."

I shrug. "Whatever. It's none of my business."

He unfolds his legs and stands up. "I want to."

I look him in the eye. "So tell me."

"You remember Pigeon's story, and Candy's—and my parents' whole weird name thing."

"Yeah. I remember. You named yourselves."

"Not really. It's more like they named us after getting to know us a little." He gets quiet. "It's not the same thing."

"Look, you don't have to tell me the story," I say, punching the elevator button a few more times.

"No, I do."

The elevator comes. I look at Safer.

"So the first part is that when I was a kid, I worried a lot."

"About what?"

"About a lot of things."

"Like what?"

"Bugs," Safer says. "Lightning. Elevators. Strangers. Airplanes. Green food. Buses. Germs. Blood. Losing teeth."

"Okay. I get the idea."

"And most of all," he says, talking fast, "I was afraid of the dark. So bedtime was like this really big deal for me. I always made my mom read me like seventeen books, and sing five songs, and bring me two glasses of water. And after all that she would say goodnight. And she always said it the same way."

"Yeah?"

He takes a long breath. "Yeah. She'd say, 'Good night, sleep tight, you're safe.' And then she'd go in the other room to read or whatever, and a minute later I'd call out, 'Safer! Safer!'"

"Oh."

"Yeah, so that's the story." Safer looks exhausted. "Now you know the truth."

"Now I know *what* truth?"

"That I'm afraid of everything."

I don't say anything.

"And I always have been."

"Safer?"

"Yeah?"

"Is that the real reason you don't take the elevator? Because you're afraid of it?"

"Yeah. I've been scared of elevators forever."

"And that's why you don't—go out much? Like to DeMarco's, even?"

"Yeah. I'm kind of an inside person, mostly. I mean, I do go outside, when I have to. I just prefer it inside."

"Don't your parents make you go out?"

"My parents are a little unusual, Georges. My mom is into table manners. But other than that, they're not very bossy."

I push the elevator button again, and the door slides open in front of us. Safer steps back. "I should probably go," I say, and I get in and watch the door close.

But when the elevator opens on the third floor, Safer is waiting there.

I go to our door and slide my key into the lock—smooth as silk.

"Safer?"

"Yeah?"

"Is there anything you aren't afraid of?"

"Yeah, a few things." He smiles. "I'm not afraid of dogs."

"Or dog slobber," I say. "Or avian flu."

"Right." He looks at me. "What about you, Georges? Is there anything *you're* afraid of? Or like, worried about?"

"What do you mean?"

"What I said. Are you afraid of anything?"

Am I afraid of anything? Yes, I am afraid of something.

There is one thing I am horribly, disgustingly afraid of. Something that I think could never heal. Something that would not stop hurting no matter how old I get or how big my big picture is.

"I have to go," I tell Safer.

"Wait," Safer says. "I know about your—"

I shut the door on him and walk straight into the bathroom, where I lie on the floor. I hike up the back of my shirt so that I can feel the cold tiles against my skin and I stare at the light fixture on the ceiling. There is a way in which I don't exist while I'm lying here. My brain thinks about the cold and the light and nothing else, and not one person on the planet knows exactly where I am.

There's a knock at the door.

Not the apartment door.

The bathroom door.

"I know you're in there," Safer says.

I stay where I am. "Don't you know you aren't supposed to barge in through people's front doors?" Of course he doesn't. This is Safer I'm talking to.

"I didn't come through the door," he tells me. "I came through the window."

Figures.

"I went through Dan's apartment—upstairs, I mean. Out onto his fire escape and down a flight into your bedroom. That's how I left you that note under your pillow the first night."

"Dan?" I say. "Don't you mean 'Mr. X, the mysterious killer'? Who wears black and has sharp knives and probably carts dead people around in suitcases? And doesn't own a baseball cap with a fish on it? Or have a dog?"

"I'm his dog walker. I have his keys because I was watering his plants and getting his mail while he was out of town."

"Good to know," I say to the bathroom ceiling.

"I'm sorry," Safer says. "I thought we were having fun."

"Because it's fun to be lied to?"

"It was a game, Georges. It was your idea, kind of."

"My idea?"

"The Spy Club. You left a note on that old sign in the basement. Pigeon put that up there like five years ago. He always has these ideas for clubs. He used to, anyway. But the Spy Club never took off, until you came. I went down to put our laundry in the dryer and there was this note, out of nowhere. Remember? You wrote, *What time?*"

"That was my *dad.*" "Yeah, but I didn't know that. And then you came to the meeting. I was glad."

"Well, I'm happy I could help you out by being your idiot."

"I never thought you were an idiot. I thought you kind of knew. The whole body-in-a-suitcase thing? I stole that from an old Alfred Hitchcock movie I saw with my dad. My dad is really into movies."

"Thanks for clueing me in. Better late than never."

There's no sound for a minute, and I wonder whether he's left. But then he says, "My mom says if your dad has to go to the hospital, you can come for dinner if you want. Just, you know, to be with people."

"People who lie?"

"Okay. Should I just go?"

"Feel free to use the front door."

Safer has completely messed up the nonexistent feeling I was going for. After I hear the front door close, I head out to the television for some *America's Funniest Home Videos*. I go to the refrigerator for a string cheese, and I see Dad's note next to the Post-it with the telephone number at the hospital:

Visiting Mom. Call my cell for dinner plan.

I'm staring at the note for a weirdly long time, and then I get this taste in my mouth, a horrible taste of something much worse than Mr. Landau's chemical ribbon.

I drink a ton of water from the kitchen faucet, but the taste won't go away. I unwrap a string cheese but I can't eat it. I hold on to it and watch my videos, which aren't that funny anymore because I've seen them so many times. I know exactly who is about to roll down a hill or fall off a slide or get scared by a fake rat and start screaming. I know whose cat accidentally plays three seconds of Beethoven on the piano.

I go to the machine and push the Eject button. Instantly, all of it is gone: the clapping, the laughing, the host who smiles literally every second of the show. The DVD slides toward me, and I take it with two fingers and stare at Mom's writing:

Smile, Pickle. I love you.

That taste is still in my mouth. I know what it is. It's the taste of pretending. It's the taste of lying. It's the taste of a game that is over.

The muscle at the back of my throat flexes, again and again, and I can't stop it. For a second I think I might throw up, and then I realize that no, I'm going to cry.

I cry on my bed that is Dad's old bed. At first the taste in my mouth gets even worse; it's something thick and awful, like tar all inside my mouth and down my throat and up my nose. I cry right through it because I have no choice, and it's like choking.

But then the taste changes. Something is washing the tar away. I'm disappeared into the crying, and I'm trying to stay that way, because it feels so good to disappear, to just lie there on the bed letting my body take over and get rid of every part of that awful taste.

I don't want to think, I don't want to hear my thoughts. Instead, I'm feeding myself images, sad and sadder—Mom kissing me and pushing the hair out of my eyes, Dallas Llewellyn's foot in my stomach, Mom's suitcase by the front door and Dad running back to the bedroom for her pillow, the look on his face with that pillow tucked under his arm—and it's like striking match after match, each one bursting into flame and sending a sharp smell straight up my nose into my brain. The pictures are making me heave and rock until they slow down and then I can't come up with any more pictures, and the taste of my crying is light and clear and makes me think of the ocean at Cape Cod. I want to keep it going and going—*Keep going,* I tell myself. But just those two words, that one half-thought, breaks the spell, and I can tell that it'll be over soon, and then I'm suddenly just me again for the first moment since I stood in front of the television wondering if I was going to puke or what.

Mom fainted in the kitchen of our house two weeks ago while she was packing our cookbooks for the move. Her head made a horrible sound when it hit the floor.

Dad ran over and yelled, "She's burning up, she's burning up!" like he was shouting it to the whole house.

Mom woke up and told Dad to stay calm. No ambulance, she told him. We were going to drive to the hospital. She'd need some things. And she wanted a pillow, her own pillow. She was saying all the things Mom would say, in a shaky voice that sounded like anything but Mom.

At the hospital, they took her away and the nurses brought us into a special room to wait. Then Dad disappeared, and I waited and waited while nurses buzzed around. Every time one of them came near me I thought it was bad news and my heart started busting its way up through my throat, but it was always a paper cup of ice and ginger ale, or a little bag of pretzels dropped into my lap with a wink, and no answer to the question I was too scared to ask.

Finally, finally, Dad showed up to tell me that the doctors said Mom had a serious infection, and she caught it from one of her patients in intensive care. They had medicine for it, Dad said, but the medicine was at the hospital, and it was the kind that went from a bag through a tube into the bloodstream, so Mom would have to stay here. They needed to watch her. For a week. Or maybe two.

Mom would have told me the actual exact name of it, I remember thinking. She would have said something like "Georges, I've got the X virus, strain Z. It's a bad one, but there's medicine for it, and I won't die on you." But no one said any of that.

"It won't be so bad," Dad told me. "It'll be just like when she's working a lot of double shifts. And before we know it, she'll be back home. Okay?"

I nodded, squeezing three little bags of pretzels.

A nurse came in and said I could see Mom now. She was in her own room right down the hall.

We started walking.

And that's when I freaked out.

I lie on the bed holding the string cheese and the DVD with Mom's words on it, just breathing. Then I go to the bathroom and wash my face. I look at myself in the mirror but I don't ask myself to smile.

I get the phone and call Dad. I don't need to look at that note on the fridge because I have memorized Mom's number at the hospital from all the times I decided not to call it.

Dad answers the phone. "I want to come with you tomorrow," I tell him. "I'm spending the day with you guys. At the hospital."

There's a silence. "Really?" he says. "That's wonderful. I'll call school in the morning, and we'll go first thing."

"Can I talk to her? Can she talk?"

"Of course she can talk. She's doing great. But she's sleeping now. Let me see if I can get her up."

"No, don't. Don't wake her up."

"Georges? How was school?"

"Better," I tell him. "It was better."

Dad says he'll leave the hospital in an hour and we'll have dinner together, but I tell him to stay where he is, that I'm fine. He says he'll be home before bedtime. I think about making some eggs. But the next thing I know my feet are taking me out the door and up the stairs and my hand is pushing Safer's doorbell.

I hear footsteps. "Hello?" It's Safer's voice, through the door.

"Where's Candy?" I ask. "Did your doorman go on vacation?"

"Did I hear a 'knock, knock'?"

"Safer, I know it's you."

But he just says it again: "Did I hear a 'knock, knock'?"

Fine. I'll play. "Knock, knock," I say.

"Who's there?" Safer says.

"Interrupting cow." And I start sucking in air, because I'm going to blow Safer away. When he starts to say "Interrupting cow, who?" I'm going to give him the longest, loudest MOO in the history of the planet.

But Safer doesn't say "Interrupting cow, who?" Instead, the door opens, and there he is. "Come in, interrupting cow," he says. "Come on in."

How to Land a Plane

In our house, up on my fire escape, my mom used to tell me bedtime stories when I was little.

A lot of the time it was this one:

My mother went to England when she was sixteen years old—her one and only trip to Europe. It was part of a youth group trip, and she was super-excited. She sat by the window on the airplane—it was her first time on a plane—and she watched the earth pull away, watched the cars, the houses, and the buildings shrink until they were dots of color, part of a giant mosaic that she would not have recognized as her own city.

"I'd seen my world close up, but never from a distance. It's like the paintings." She would nudge me with an elbow. "By the painter who painted the little dots that made beautiful pictures."

"I know," I would say.

"What's his name?"

"Sir Ott," I would say, because I wanted her to go on with the story.

"What's his *first* name?"

"Georges." She always kissed my forehead when I said that.

The mosaic of my mother's city gave way to blue water that darkened as they flew toward night, until everything outside turned black and all she could see in the window was her own reflection. They brought food but she couldn't eat. She was too excited. She stared at her face in the window and thought, *Here is me, going to England; here is me, crossing the ocean; here is me, a dot in the sky.*

"How was it?" I asked her once.

"How was what?"

"How was it to be a dot in the sky? Like a nothing."

"I didn't feel like a nothing. I felt—*full.*"

"But you just said you couldn't eat."

She said she felt full of whatever it was that was about to happen to her.

After a long time, she saw something else through the window. She saw lights. Not big bright lights like in Times Square, but a million tiny lights that glowed.

She would close her eyes when she told this part.

"It was as if heavy clothes, embroidered with glowing threads of gold and red, had been tossed down by a giant or a god, and were just floating there, on top of the water."

And it was beautiful, flying over that.

But as the plane flew lower and the pressure built in her ears, she found that she did not want to land. She wanted to stay above all of it, partly because it was beautiful, and partly because she understood that all the time she had been in the air, her connection to home had been stretching like a rubber band. It had stretched very far, so far that she was afraid that when the plane touched down, the rubber band would break, and a part of her life would be over.

"Isn't that silly?" she'd say. "Where did I get that idea?"

My mother's bedtime stories were not like other people's.

And that's how it was for me that night two weeks ago, when the nurse finally came to the waiting room and said I could see Mom. Walking down the hospital hallway, matching my steps to Dad's, I suddenly did not want to see her, to actually arrive at the door to her room, because as long as I did not get there, I was still in the part of my life when she was not sick. And that's why I refused to go into her room, why I started crying and ran to the elevators, and why I said I would never go back. I decided to do exactly what Dad said, to pretend that she was just at work, that none of it was happening.

But obviously Mom *had* left on that plane, a long time before it landed in London, the same way I had left the place where Mom was not sick the very second that she fainted in our kitchen.

The last part of Mom's plane trip was a long moment when the plane was gliding over the runway in London, just barely off the ground. The sun was up, and the world was normal-size again, but the wheels had not yet touched the earth. She suddenly knew everything would be all right. And that, she said, was a beautiful feeling.

Little of Both

I hate the hospital as soon as we walk into it. First, I hate the round coffee kiosk on the first floor where Dad stops to buy a cappuccino, because it's fake cheerful, and then I hate the elevators that stop on every floor and take forever to get to nine. They ding and buzz and we have to wait while things are wheeled in and out. I hate that.

"Here he is!" a nurse says when we check in at the desk on Mom's ward. "And looking every bit as serious as his mother warned."

Her accent is nice—I don't hate it—but I can't smile back at her. Now that I'm here, I just want to see Mom.

Dad's hand is on the back of my neck. "Hi, Sophia. Anything we need to know?"

"Nothing at all," she says. "It's been a good morning, even better than good. And I've told them all to leave you alone, or else." She raises one fist and shakes it, but she isn't doing it for my benefit, and this is another thing I don't hate.

Dad smiles. "Great. We'll head back, then."

"Don't think I don't know the coffee is for her!" Sophia calls after us.

I glance up at Dad's face. "She's not supposed to drink caffeine yet," Dad says. "But you know what they say—doctors and nurses make the worst patients."

I match my stride to Dad's as we walk down the hall, one-two, one-two—and I tell myself that if we can get all the way to Mom's room without having to stop for a passing lunch-tray cart or a sliding door, it will be a good sign.

"Right here," Dad says. His hand is still on my neck. We turn.

Mom is on the bed, on top of the covers. She's got on jeans and a T-shirt. She looks normal, like her regular self. But when she reaches for me, there's a tube connected to her arm.

She follows my eyes. "Don't worry about this thing," she says, swatting at the tube. "Just more antibiotics.

"I can't stand not hugging you for one more second," Mom says. Her arms are out again, and Dad pushes the back of my neck, just a little bit.

I walk to the bed slowly, thinking about where to put my arms. I wonder if there are other tubes, hidden ones that I might accidentally touch or break. But when I get close enough Mom's hands just take me and pull me in, and she's a lot stronger than I thought she would be.

We don't try to catch up. We don't pour our hearts out. Instead, we watch a show on Mom's television. She makes room for me in the bed on the side without any tubes, and Dad pulls a chair up close. We laugh at every joke, and once in a while Mom kisses me, and once in a while she reaches for Dad's coffee and takes a sip.

No one comes in to remind us that we are in a hospital, and the machines on the walls and the metal bed rails kind of disappear for a while. During commercials, I take things in and Mom watches me.

"This is where I keep your notes," she says. And she shows me a notebook with my Scrabble messages. She's written them out, my words and hers, which Dad spelled out for me after I fell asleep.

She takes my hand and turns it so that the blue dot on my palm is facing up.

"What's this?"

"Long story," I tell her.

"Good story or bad story?"

I don't know how to answer that.

She squeezes my hand. "Little of both?"

"Yeah," I tell her. "A little of both."

"Tell me next time?"

"Sure."

When Dad and I get home from the hospital, I call Safer. He answers on the first ring.

I tell him to come downstairs and to bring his notebook. "We're going to make a list," I say.

It's a list of everything Safer is not afraid of.

The Scout

It's obviously pretty strange to have your first day of school on a Thursday in June when there are only three weeks left in the whole year, but it seems like there's never been anything extremely normal about Safer's family. Candy has decided to join the fourth grade, and she does not plan to wait until September.

"Everyone makes such a big deal about the last day of school," she tells me, stuffing her lunch into her new backpack. "I don't want to miss it."

Which makes Safer nod like he totally gets it. He holds his flask out to me. "Coffee?"

"Safer, what's really *in* there?"

"Coffee!" he says, looking insulted. He takes a swig from the flask.

"Safer," his mom says, "I wish you'd get bored with that thing already. It's heck to wash."

She's taking pictures of Candy in her first-day-of-school outfit, which is jeans and a T-shirt. Candy was going to wear her overalls, but when she asked me if other kids wear overalls to school, I had to tell her not so much. She said she didn't mind being different, but maybe not on her very first day. She's going to wear them tomorrow.

Safer's mom clicks away with her camera while Candy zips up her bag and says she's ready. Safer says he's ready too. Because it's his job to walk her.

We've been working on Safer's list for the past couple of weeks, adding things one by one.

First, we walked to the corner and back with Ty and Lucky, Safer gripping a leash in each hand.

Then we walked to Bennie's with Candy, who was running low on Starbursts. She bought three packs and opened them all in the store, picking out the orange ones and splitting them between me and Safer while talking to Bennie about when the Mallomars will be delivered in the fall. It turns out that the Mallomar is a seasonal cookie.

Last weekend, Safer and I made it all the way to DeMarco's with Pigeon. "You know, the pizza really is better straight out of the oven," Safer said after finishing his second slice. And Pigeon hugged him.

The day before yesterday, Safer and I took our longest walk yet, just the two of us, to my old house. I showed him the porch and the big crack in the sidewalk where I chipped my tooth, and I pointed to my old bedroom window and told him about my fire escape. I wanted him to see it, because that house was like a friend to me. But Safer is a better one.

When Safer's mom goes into her office to put her camera away, Candy quickly pops a giant SweeTart into her mouth. Dad took me and Safer on the D train yesterday to buy them for her at the newsstand on the Fifty-Ninth Street platform. It was her first-day-of-school present, from us.

"It's about time," Safer said on the subway. "I'm pretty sure Candy's wanted to go to school forever. She used to stand at the window and count the yellow buses."

I didn't say what I was thinking, that maybe she had stayed at home for his sake, but now she doesn't need to anymore.

I tell Candy and Safer I'll meet them in the lobby, and then I run down to our apartment for my backpack and almost slam into Mom, who's getting her sneakers on by the door.

"Oops," she says. "Are you leaving? It's later than I thought. I'm supposed to meet Dad at some kind of vintage-appliance warehouse."

I'm guessing that pretty soon we'll have a weird old stove, like Safer's.

"Drive safely," I tell her.

"Oh, I'm walking," she says, pointing at her sneakers. "Gotta stay in shape—tomorrow I'll be on my feet all day."

Mom's been busy too, getting back to normal. She goes back to work tomorrow. No doubles for a while, though. She promised.

When I get downstairs, Safer and Candy are waiting in the lobby chairs, and the three of us head out. I've told Bob to wait for us by the front doors at school, and he's right there when we turn the corner, flipping his blue Sharpie into the air and catching it.

"Ready?" he asks.

"Hold out your hand," I tell Candy.

Bob draws Candy's blue dot, making a perfect circle and then coloring it in.

When he's done, she looks at it up close. "So what does this mean again?"

Bob tells her. "It means you're not alone. No matter what."

She nods. She looks smaller out here in front of the school than she does at home. Kids are starting to swarm all around us, heading into the building. Candy tightens her ponytail.

"I'll walk you to your class," I say. "She has Ms. Diamatis," I tell Bob.

"That's who I had," he says to Candy. "I hope you know your times tables. Ms. Diamatis is really into multiplication."

"Of course she knows her times tables!" Safer says. "I bet she knows them better than anyone in the whole school." Candy gives Safer a big grateful smile, and I notice that her teeth are a little purple around the edges.

Safer turns to me, mock-offended. "Does he think I would send my scout in unprepared?"

"Don't start," I tell him.

Safer is considering school himself. He says that Candy is his scout, that if she reports that school is okay and confirms where all the exits are, he might start eighth grade with me and Bob in September.

Or maybe ninth grade, he says, *next* September.

He's kidding about the exits. I think.

Last period. Gym. The whiteboard is blank. Ms. Warner says we can pick what game to play. The Blue Team carries the vote with capture the flag. Our jailbreaks are getting better and better.

After the bell, Ms. Warner waves me over.

"I met your friend today," she says, because I've already told Ms. Warner to look out for Candy. "Great kid."

"Don't try to give her any nicknames," I say.

She grins. "You got it, G. No nicknames."

I take a deep breath. "Tell me the truth. Do you really hate your job?"

She looks at me. "This is pretty much my dream job, G."

I knew it.

She holds up one hand. "High five?"

It isn't Friday. But rules are made to be broken.

Thanks

Thank you, talented, busy friends and family who gave your time to read my drafts, answer my questions, and share your magic: Randi Kish, Deborah Heiligman, Donna Freitas, Daphne Grab, Judy Blundell, Deborah Stead, David Levithan, and Karen Romano Young. Without your friendship, both my work and my life would be diminished.

Thank you, Caroline Meckler, Dana Carey, and Robert Warren, editors full of greatness.

Thank you, Kate Gartner and Yan Nascimbene, for making this book beautiful to me.

Thank you, Colleen Fellingham and Barbara Perris, for lending your wise minds and eagle eyes to this work.

Thank you, Joan DeMayo, Tracy Lerner, Adrienne Waintraub, Lisa Nadel, and Judith Haut, smart and fabulous women with the difficult job of getting books into the hands of real people.

Thank you, Megan Looney, Mary Van Akin, and Tamar Schwartz, for your insight, your energy, and your time.

Thank you, Chip Gibson, for your unflagging support and your irrepressible spirit.

Thank you, Faye Bender, my secret agent, for being wonderful.

Thank you, Wendy Lamb, my editor, my friend, and an extraordinary woman who makes dreams come true.

Rebecca Stead is the author of two previous novels, *First Light* and *When You Reach Me*, which was a *New York Times* bestseller and winner of the Newbery Medal and the *Boston Globe–Horn Book* Award for fiction. She lives in New York City with her family.

REBECCA STEAD

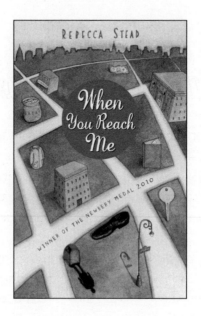

If you've enjoyed *Liar & Spy* – try this excerpt from
Rebecca Stead's other brilliant novel; *When You Reach Me*.

Things You Keep in a Box

So Mom got the postcard today. It says *Congratulations* in big curly letters, and at the very top is the address of Studio TV-15 on West 58th Street. After three years of trying, she has actually made it. She's going to be a contestant on *The $20,000 Pyramid*, which is hosted by Dick Clark.

On the postcard there's a list of things to bring. She needs some extra clothes in case she wins and makes it to another show, where they pretend it's the next day even though they really tape five in one afternoon. Barrettes are optional, but she should definitely bring some with her. Unlike me, Mom has glossy red hair that bounces around and might obstruct America's view of her small freckled face.

And then there's the date she's supposed to show up, scrawled in blue pen on a line at the bottom of the card: *April 27, 1979.* Just like you said.

I check the box under my bed, which is where I've kept your notes these past few months. There it is, in your tiny handwriting: *April 27th: Studio TV-15,* the words all jerky-looking, like you wrote them on the subway. Your last "proof."

I still think about the letter you asked me to write. It nags at me, even though you're gone and there's no one to give it to anymore. Sometimes I work on it in my head, trying to map out the story you asked me to tell, about everything that happened this past fall and winter. It's all still there, like a movie I can watch when I want to. Which is never.

Things That Go Missing

Mom has swiped a big paper calendar from work and Scotch-taped the month of April to the kitchen wall. She used a fat green marker, also swiped from work, to draw a pyramid on April 27, with dollar signs and exclamation points all around it. She went out and bought a fancy egg timer that can accurately measure a half minute. They don't have fancy egg timers in the supply closet at her office.

April twenty-seventh is also Richard's birthday. Mom wonders if that's a good omen. Richard is Mom's boyfriend. He and I are going to help Mom practice every single night, which is why I'm sitting at my desk instead of watching after-school TV, which is a birthright of every latchkey child. "Latchkey child" is a name for a kid with keys who hangs out alone af- ter school until a grown-up gets home to make din- ner. Mom hates that expression. She says it reminds her of dungeons, and must have been invented by someone strict and awful with an unlimited child- care budget. "Probably someone German," she says, glaring at Richard, who is German but not strict or awful.

It's possible. In Germany, Richard says, I would be one of the *Schlüsselkinder*, which means "key children."

"You're lucky," he tells me. "Keys are power. Some of us have to come knocking." It's true that he doesn't have a key. Well, he has a key to *his* apartment, but not to ours.

Richard looks the way I picture guys on sailboats—tall, blond, and very tucked-in, even on weekends. Or maybe I picture guys on sailboats that way because Richard loves to sail. His legs are very long, and they don't really fit under our kitchen table, so he has to sit kind of sideways, with his knees pointing out toward the hall. He looks especially big next to Mom, who's short and so tiny she has to buy her belts in the kids' department and make an extra hole in her watchband so it won't fall off her arm.

Mom calls Richard Mr. Perfect because of how he looks and how he knows everything. And every time she calls him Mr. Perfect, Richard taps his right knee. He does that because his right leg is shorter than his left one. All his right-foot shoes have two-inch platforms nailed to the bottom so that his legs match. In bare feet, he limps a little.

"You should be grateful for that leg," Mom tells him. "It's the only reason we let you come around." Richard has been "coming around" for almost two years now.

* * *

We have exactly twenty-one days to get Mom ready for the game show. So instead of watching television, I'm copying words for her practice session tonight. I write each word on one of the white index cards Mom swiped from work. When I have seven words, I bind the cards together with a rubber band she also swiped from work.

I hear Mom's key in the door and flip over my word piles so she can't peek.

"Miranda?" She clomps down the hall—she's on a clog kick lately—and sticks her head in my room. "Are you starving? I thought we'd hold dinner for Richard."

"I can wait." The truth is I've just eaten an entire bag of Cheez Doodles. After-school junk food is another fundamental right of the latchkey child. I'm sure this is true in Germany, too.

"You're sure you're not hungry? Want me to cut up an apple for you?"

"What's a kind of German junk food?" I ask her. "Wiener crispies?"

She stares at me. "I have no idea. Why do you ask?"

"No reason."

"Do you want the apple or not?"

"No, and get out of here—I'm doing the words for later."

"Great." She smiles and reaches into her coat pocket. "Catch." She lobs something toward me, and I grab what turns out to be a bundle of brand-new markers in rainbow colors, held together with a fat rubber band. She clomps back toward the kitchen.

Richard and I figured out a while ago that the more stuff Mom swipes from the office supply closet, the more she's hating work. I look at the markers for a second and then get back to my word piles.

Mom has to win this money.

Things You Hide

I was named after a criminal. Mom says that's a dramatic way of looking at things, but sometimes the truth is dramatic.

"The name Miranda stands for people's rights," she said last fall, when I was upset because Robbie B. had told me during gym that I was named after a kidnapper.

I had left my keys at school and waited two and a half hours at Belle's Market on Amsterdam Avenue for Mom to get home from work. I didn't mind the waiting so much. I helped Belle out around the store for a while. And I had my book, of course.

"Still reading that same book?" Belle asked, once I had settled into my folding chair next to the cash register to read. "It's looking pretty beat-up."

"I'm not *still* reading it," I told her. "I'm reading it *again*." I had probably read it a hundred times, which was why it looked so beat-up.

"Okay," Belle said, "so let's hear something about this book. What's the first line? I never judge a book by the cover," she said. "I judge by the first line."

I knew the first line of my book without even looking. "It was a dark and stormy night," I said.

She nodded. "Classic. I like that. What's the story about?"

I thought for a second. "It's about a girl named Meg—her dad is missing, and she goes on this trip to another planet to save him."

"And? Does she have a boyfriend?"

"Sort of," I said. "But that's not really the point."

"How old is she?"

"Twelve." The truth is that my book doesn't say how old Meg is, but I am twelve, so she feels twelve to me. When I first got the book I was eleven, and she felt eleven.

"Oh, twelve," Belle said. "Plenty of time for boyfriends, then. Why don't you start from the beginning?"

"Start what from the beginning?"

"The story. Tell me the story. From the beginning."

So I started telling her the story of my book, not reading it to her, just telling her about it, starting with the first scene, where Meg wakes up at night, afraid of a thunderstorm.

While she listened, Belle made me a turkey sandwich and gave me about ten chewable vitamin Cs because she thought I sounded nasal. When she went to the bathroom, I sneaked a little bunch of grapes, which I love but can't ever have, because Mom doesn't like the way the grape pickers are treated in California and she refuses to buy them.

* * *

When she finally got there, Mom hugged Belle and told her, "I owe you," like I was some repulsive burden instead of the person who had very helpfully unpacked three boxes of green bananas and scoured the refrigerated section for expired dairy items. Then Mom bought a box of strawberries, even though I know she thinks Belle's strawberries are overpriced and not very good. She calls them SSO's, which stands for "strawberry-shaped objects."

"Where did Robbie B. get the dumb idea that anyone would name her own daughter after a murderer?" Mom asked. Our building was still half a block away, but her key was already in her hand. Mom doesn't like to fumble around in front of the building looking like a target for muggers.

"Not a murderer," I said. "A kidnapper. Robbie B.'s dad is a prosecutor. He says the Miranda warnings were named for a guy named Mr. Miranda who committed some horrible crime. Is that true?"

"Technically? Maybe. The Miranda warnings are essential, you know. People need to know that they have the right to remain silent and the right to an attorney. What kind of justice system would we have without—"

" 'Maybe' meaning 'yes'?"

"—and then there's Shakespeare. He invented the name Miranda, you know, for *The Tempest*."

It made perfect sense now that I thought about it: Mom wanted to be a criminal defense lawyer—she started law school and almost finished her first year, but then I was born and she had to quit. Now she's a paralegal, except she works at a really small law office where she has to be the receptionist and the secretary too. Richard is one of the lawyers. They do a lot of free work for poor people, sometimes even for criminals. But I never dreamed she would name me after one.

Mom unlocked the lobby door, which is iron and glass and must weigh three hundred pounds, and she pushed hard to swing it open, her heels slipping on the tile floor. When we were inside, she leaned against the other side of the door until she heard the click that means the lock has caught. When the door swings shut by itself, it usually doesn't lock, which drives Mom nuts and is one of the things the landlord won't fix.

"So? Was he a kidnapper or not?" I punched the button for the elevator.

"Okay, you win," Mom said. "I named you after a monster, Mira. I'm sorry. If you don't like your name, you are welcome to change it."

That was so Mom. She didn't understand that a person gets attached to a person's name, that something like this might come as a shock.

Upstairs, she threw her coat on a kitchen chair, filled the spaghetti pot with water, and put it on to boil. She was wearing an orange turtleneck and a denim skirt with purple and black striped tights.

"Nice tights," I snorted. Or I tried to snort, anyway. I'm not exactly sure how, though people in books are always doing it.

She leaned against the sink and flipped through the mail. "You already hassled me about the tights this morning, Mira."

"Oh." She was usually still in bed when I left for school, so I didn't get to appreciate her outfit until she got home from work. "Nice nail polish, then." Her nails were electric blue. She must have done them at her desk that day.

She rolled her eyes. "Are you mad about waiting at Belle's? I was super busy—I couldn't just leave."

"No. I like it at Belle's." I wondered whether she'd done her nails before, after, or during her super busy afternoon.

"You could have gone to Sal's, you know." Sal and his mom, Louisa, live in the apartment below ours. Sal used to be my best friend.

"I said I *like* it at Belle's."

"Still. I think we should hide a key in the fire hose, for the next time."

So after dinner we hid our spare key inside the nozzle of the dusty, folded-up fire hose in the stairwell. The hose is all cracked-looking and about a hundred years old, and Mom always says that if there's an actual fire it will be of no use whatsoever and we'll have to jump out the window into the neighbor's garden. It's a good thing we live on the second floor.

You asked me to mention the key. If I ever do decide to write your letter, which I probably won't, this is the story I would tell you.

The Speed Round

There are two parts to *The $20,000 Pyramid*. Mom calls the first part the speed round because it's all about speed. Contestants try to make their celebrity partners guess seven common words by giving clues. So if the first word is "fork," a contestant might say, "You use this to put food in your mouth—not a spoon but a . . ."

If he has a brain, which Mom says he might not, the celebrity partner will say "Fork!" and then there'll be a ding and the next word will show up on a little hidden screen. Each team gets thirty seconds for seven words.

Then the little screens swivel around, and it's the celebrities' turn to give the clues and the contestants' turn to guess. Another seven words, another thirty seconds. Then the screens swivel back, and the contestants give the clues again.

There are a possible twenty-one points in the speed round, and a perfect score earns a cash bonus of twenty-one hundred dollars. But the most important thing is just to beat the other team, because the team that wins the speed round goes to the Winner's Circle, and the Winner's Circle is where the big money is.

There isn't a lot of time for practice tonight because it's tenant-meeting night. Once a month, the neighbors sit in our living room and complain while Mom takes notes in shorthand. Most people don't bother to come. It's always the old folks, who don't get asked to go many places and are mad that there isn't more heat. Sal's mom, Louisa, works in a nursing home, and she says old people can never get enough heat.

After the meetings, during which Mr. Nunzi has usually burned a new hole in our couch with his cigarette, Mom always writes a letter to the landlord and sends a copy to some city agency that's supposed to care whether we have hot water, if the lobby door locks, and that the elevator keeps getting stuck between floors. But nothing ever changes.

Our doorbell is going to start ringing any minute. Mom is running through a few speed rounds with Richard while I make lemonade from frozen concentrate and open the Oreos.

Louisa knocks her regular knock and I answer the door with the plate of cookies. She takes an Oreo and sighs. She's wearing jeans with her white nurse shoes, which she kicks off by the door. She hates these meetings but comes out of loyalty to Mom. And someone has to watch Mr. Nunzi's cigarette to make sure he doesn't accidentally set our apartment on fire.

"Lemonade?" I ask. I refuse to play waitress during Mom's get-togethers, but I'll pour Louisa a drink anytime.

"Lemonade sounds lovely." She follows me to the kitchen.

Just as I put the glass in her hand, the doorbell buzzes for about a minute straight. Why, why, *why* do they have to hold the button down forever?

"Old people," Louisa says, as if she can read my mind. "They're so used to being ignored." She grabs two more cookies and goes to answer the door. Louisa doesn't normally eat what she calls processed foods, but she says she could never get through a tenant meeting without Oreos.

Fifteen minutes later, Mom is sitting on the living room floor, writing furiously as everyone takes turns saying that the elevator is dirty, there are cigarette butts on the stairs, and the dryer in the basement melted somebody's elastic-waist pants.

I lean against the wall in the hallway and watch her hold up one finger to signal Mrs. Bindocker to slow down. Once Mrs. Bindocker gets going, not even Mom's shorthand can keep up with her.

Mom cried the first time she saw our apartment. The whole place was filthy, she says. The wood floors were "practically black," the windows were "caked with dirt," and the walls were smeared with something she "didn't even want to think about." Always in those same words.

I was there that day—in a little bucket-seat baby carrier. It was cold out, and she had a new coat on. There were no hangers in the closets, and she didn't want to put the coat down on the dirty floor or drape it over one of the peeling, hissing radiators, so she carried it while she went from room to room, telling herself it wasn't so awful.

At this point in the story, I used to try to think of someplace she could have put her coat, if only she had thought of it.

"Why didn't you drape it over the rod in the hall closet?" I'd ask.

"Dusty," she'd say.

"On the windowsill in the kitchen?"

"Dusty."

"What about over the top of the bedroom door?"

"Couldn't reach," she'd say, "*and* dusty."

What Mom did that day almost twelve years ago was put her coat back on, pick up my bucket seat, and walk to a store, where she bought a mop, some soap, garbage bags, a roll of sticky shelf paper, sponges, a bottle of window spray, and paper towels.

Back home, she dumped everything out on the floor. Then she folded her coat and slid it into the empty bag from the store. She hung the bag on a doorknob and cleaned the apartment all afternoon. I knew enough, she says, to snuggle down in my bucket seat and take a very long nap.

She met Louisa, who didn't have a husband either, in the lobby on that first day. They were both taking garbage to the big cans out front. Louisa was holding Sal. Sal had been crying, but when he saw me, he stopped.

I know all this because I used to ask to hear the story over and over: the story of the day I met Sal.

Things That Kick

Losing Sal was like a long list of bad things, and some-where in the top half of the list was the fact that I had to walk home alone past the crazy guy on our corner.

He showed up around the beginning of the school year, when Sal and I still walked home from school together. A few kids called him Quack, short for Quackers, or they called him Kicker because he used to do these sudden kicks into the street, like he was trying to punt one of the cars speeding up Amsterdam Avenue. Sometimes he shook his fist at the sky and yelled crazy stuff like "What's the burn scale? Where's the dome?" and then he threw his head back and laughed these loud, crazy laughs, so everyone could see that he had about thirty fillings in his teeth. And he was always on our corner, sometimes sleeping with his head under the mailbox.

"Don't call him Quack," Mom said. "That's an awful name for a human being."

"Even a human being who's quackers?"

"I don't care. It's still awful."

"Well, what do *you* call him?"

"I don't call him anything," she said, "but I think of him as the laughing man."

Back when I still walked home with Sal, it was easier to pretend that the laughing man didn't scare me, because Sal was pretending too. He tried not to show it, but he freaked when he saw the laughing man shaking his fist at the sky and kicking his leg out into traffic. I could tell by the way Sal's face kind of froze. I know all of his expressions.

I used to think of Sal as being a part of me: Sal and Miranda, Miranda and Sal. I knew he wasn't really, but that's the way it felt.

When we were too little for school, Sal and I went to day care together at a lady's apartment down the block. She had picked up some carpet samples at a store on Amsterdam Avenue and written the kids' names on the backs. After lunch, she'd pass out these carpet squares and we'd pick our spots on the living room floor for nap time. Sal and I always lined ours up to make a rectangle.

One time, when Sal had a fever and Louisa had called in sick to her job and kept him home, the day-care lady handed me my carpet square at nap time, and then, a second later, she gave me Sal's, too.

"I know how it is, baby," she said.

And then I lay on her floor not sleeping because Sal wasn't there to press his foot against mine.

* * *

When he first showed up on our corner last fall, the laughing man was always mumbling under his breath. "Bookbag, pocketshoe, bookbag, pocketshoe."

He said it like a chant: *book*bag, *pocket*shoe, *book*bag, *pocket*shoe. And sometimes he would be hitting himself on the head with his fists. Sal and I usually tried to get really interested in our conversation and act like we didn't notice. It's crazy the things a person can pretend not to notice.

"Why do you think he sleeps like that, with his head under the mailbox?" I asked Richard back when the laughing man was brand-new and I was still trying to figure him out.

"I don't know," Richard said, looking up from the paper. "Maybe so nobody steps on his head?"

"Very funny. And what's a 'pocketshoe,' anyway?"

"Pocketshoe," he said, looking serious. "Noun: An extra shoe you keep in your pocket. In case someone steals one of yours while you're asleep with your head under the mailbox."

"Ha ha ha," I said.

"Oh, Mr. Perfect," Mom said. "You and your amazing dictionary head!" She was in one of her good moods that day.

Richard tapped his right knee and went back to his newspaper.

Things That Get Tangled

Lucky for Mom, some of the old people at the nursing home where Louisa works like to watch *The $20,000 Pyramid* at lunchtime. Louisa takes notes on every show and brings them over after work. She gets off at four, so I have time to write out the day's words on stolen index cards before Mom gets home.

Tonight, Mom and Richard are practicing in the living room. I'm supposed to be doing homework in my room, but instead I'm tying knots and I'm thinking.

It was Richard who taught me how to tie knots. He learned back when he sailed boats as a kid, and he still carries pieces of rope in his briefcase. He says that when he's trying to solve a problem at work, he takes out the ropes, ties them into knots, unties them, and then ties them again. It gets him in the right frame of mind.

Two Christmases ago, which was his first Christmas with us, Richard gave me my own set of ropes and started showing me knots. Now I can make every knot he knows, even the clove hitch, which I did backward for a few months before I got it right. So I am tying and untying knots, and seeing if it helps me solve my problem, which is you. I have no idea what you expect from me.

If you just wanted to know what happened that day this past winter, it would be easy. Not fun, but easy. But that's not what your note says. It says to write down the story of what happened *and everything that led up to it*. And, as Mom likes to say, that's a whole different bucket of poop. Except she doesn't use the word "poop."

Because even if you were still here, even if I *did* decide to write the letter, I wouldn't know where to start. The day the laughing man showed up on our corner? The day Mom and Louisa met in the lobby? The day I found your first note?

There is no answer. But if someone sat on my legs and forced me to name the day the whole true story began, I'd say it was the day Sal got punched.

Things That Stain

It happened in the fall, when Sal and I still walked home from school together every single day: one block from West End Avenue to Broadway, one block from Broadway to Amsterdam, past the laughing man on our corner, and then half a block to our lobby door.

That middle block between Broadway and Amsterdam is mostly a huge garage, where the sidewalk is all slanted, and we had to be careful when it was icy or else we'd slip right in front of the pack of boys always hanging out there. If we did fall, they'd make a really big deal out of it, staggering around laughing, and sometimes calling us names that made our hearts beat fast the rest of the way home.

The day Sal got punched, there was no ice on the ground because it was only October. I was carrying the big oak-tag *Mysteries of Science* poster I'd made at school. I had drawn big bubble letters for the title, which was *Why Do We Yawn?*

There are a lot of interesting theories about yawning. Some people think it started as a way of showing off the teeth to scare predators away, or as a way to stretch facial muscles, or to signal to the rest of the tribe that it's time to sleep. My own theory, which I included on my poster, is that yawning is a semipolite way of telling someone that they're boring everyone to death. Either that or it's a slow-motion sneeze. But no one knows for sure, which is why it's a mystery of science.

The day Sal got punched, the boys by the garage were hanging out, as usual. The day before, there had been a fight, with one of them slamming another one up against a parked car and hitting him. The kid getting hit had both his hands up like he was saying "Enough!", but every time he tried to get off the hood of that car, the other kid pushed him down and hit him again. The other boys were all jumping around and yelling and Sal and I had crossed to the other side of the street so that we wouldn't get accidentally slammed by somebody.

On the day Sal got punched, the boys were being regular, so we stayed on our usual side. But just as we started past the garage, someone moved away from the group. He took a big step toward me and Sal and blocked our way so that we had to stop. I looked up and saw a not-too-biggish kid in a green army coat. He made a fist that came up like a wave and hit Sal right in the stomach. Hard. Sal doubled over and gurgled like he was going to throw up. And then the kid whacked him across the face.

"Sal!" I yelled. I glanced over at Belle's Market on

Amsterdam, but no one was out front. Sal was bent over and frozen. The kid just stood there for a few seconds with his head tilted to one side. It seemed crazy, but it actually looked like he was reading my *Mysteries of Science* poster. Then he turned away and started strolling toward Broadway like nothing had happened.

"Sal!" I leaned over to see his face, which looked okay but had one cheek all red. "Walk," I said. "We're almost home."

Sal's feet started to move. It took me a few steps to realize that the boys weren't laughing or whistling or calling us names. They hadn't made a sound. I looked back and saw them standing there, staring after the kid in the green army coat, who was still walking in the other direction.

"Hey!" one of them yelled down the block after him. "What the hell was that?" But the kid didn't look back.

Sal was moving slowly. He squeezed the arms of the blue satin Yankees jacket Louisa got him for his birthday, and tears were dropping down his face, and I almost cried but didn't. It was my job to get him home, and we still had to get by the laughing man.

He was on our corner, marching around in a circle and doing some salutes. Sal was crying harder and walking in a hunch. Some blood had started dripping out of his nose, and he wiped it with the blue and white striped cuff of his jacket. He gagged a lot. It sounded like he really might throw up.

When he saw us, the laughing man dropped his arms to his sides and stood up straight. He reminded me of the big wooden nutcracker Louisa puts out on her kitchen table at Christmastime.

"Smart kid!" he said. He took a step toward us, and it was enough to make Sal take off running for home. I ran after him, trying to hold on to my poster and get my keys out of my jeans.

When I had gotten us into the lobby, Sal went straight to his apartment and closed the door on me. I knocked for a while, but Louisa wasn't home from work yet and he wouldn't let me in.

If I'm not wrong, this is the beginning of the story you wanted me to tell. And I didn't know it yet, but it was also the end of my friendship with Sal.

Mom's Rules for Life in
New York City

1. *Always* have your key out before you reach the front door.
2. If a stranger is hanging out in front of the building, don't *ever* go in—just keep walking around the block until he's gone.
3. Look ahead. If there's someone acting strange down the block, looking drunk or dangerous, cross to the other side of the street, but *don't* be obvious about it. Make it look like you were planning to cross the street all along.
4. *Never* show your money on the street.

I have my own trick. If I'm afraid of someone on the street, I'll turn to him (it's always a boy) and say, "Excuse me, do you happen to know what time it is?" This is my way of saying to the person, "I see you as a friend, and there is no need to hurt me or take my

stuff. Also, I don't even have a watch and I am probably not worth mugging."

So far, it's worked like gangbusters, as Richard
would say. And I've discovered that most people I'm
afraid of are actually very friendly.

Things You Wish For

"Miranda?" Mom calls from the kitchen. "We need you to keep time. This egg-timer ticking is driving me crazy."

So I watch the second hand of the kitchen clock while Richard feeds Mom clues. Then Mom gives the clues while Richard guesses.

"Can I play?" I ask after about five rounds.

"Sure. Richard, you keep time for a while." Mom stretches and peels off her purple sweatshirt. As it goes over her head, her hair falls free of the collar and bounces down around her shoulders. As usual, this makes me curse my nonexistent dad, who must be to blame for my hair, which is straight, brown, and just kind of *there*. I blame this stupid flat brown hair on my father, but otherwise I don't hold any grudges against him.

In my book, Meg is looking for her father. When she finally gets to Camazotz, which is a planet some-where near the Big Dipper where he's being held prisoner, this evil man with red eyes asks her *why* she wants him, and she says, "Didn't you ever have a father yourself? You don't want him for a *reason*. You want him because he's your *father*."

So I figure it's because I never *had* a father that I don't want one now. A person can't miss something she never had.

Richard is looking at the kitchen clock, waiting for the second hand to get to the twelve. "Okay, get ready—go!"

I look down at the first card. "Um, this is something you spread on toast," I say.

"Butter!" Mom yells.

Next card. "You drink a milk shake with this, you suck through it."

"A straw!" Mom yells.

Next. "It's leather and it holds your pants up!"

"A belt!"

"It's sweet—you drink it in winter, after you go sledding!"

"Hot chocolate!"

It's good to play, to think of nothing but the next word and to have Mom think of nothing but the next words out of my mouth. We fly through the pack of seven words.

"You're good at this," Mom says when we finish with five seconds to spare.

I'm smiling. "I really think you're going to win," I tell her.

"Don't get your hopes up," she warns. "This is just the speed round. The speed round is the easy part."

* * *

The truth is that our hopes are already up. Our wish list is stuck to the fridge with a magnet Mom stole from work:

> *Trip to China*
> *Good camera for trip to China*
> *Wall-to-wall carpeting for Miranda's room*
> *New TV*

And Richard has scribbled *Sailboat* at the bottom, though it's hard to imagine where we would park it.

That's the official list, anyway. Richard and I have our own secret plan for the money, if Mom wins it.

Things That Sneak Up
on You

The day Sal got punched, back in October, Louisa came upstairs after dinner to have a conference with Mom in her bedroom. They decided that Sal needed a mental health day, which meant he was allowed to skip school and watch TV the next day.

So the following afternoon I walked home alone. I was doing a lot of talking in my head so that I would be deep in conversation with myself by the time I got to the laughing man. I was almost to the garage when I realized someone was walking right behind me. I glanced back and saw the kid who punched Sal. He was maybe two feet away, wearing the same green army jacket he had worn the day before.

I was about to panic. I always know when I'm about to panic because my knees and neck both start to tingle. And then, before I had really decided what to do, I turned around to face him.

"Excuse me, do you happen to know what time it is?" My voice sounded almost normal. That was good.

"Let's see. . . ." He turned his head and looked back toward Broadway like maybe there was a giant clock hovering in the air right behind us. "It's three-sixteen."

I nodded like I could see the invisible clock too. "Thanks." He didn't look like he was about to hit me, but still, my heart was pounding.

He pointed. "See that big brown building? Yesterday the sun started to go behind it at three-twelve. Now it's about halfway gone." He glanced at me. "Plus, it's one day later, and it's October, so the days are getting shorter."

I stared at him. He looked down at his hand, which held a key. He pushed the other hand into his pants pocket. "I don't have a watch," he said.

"Oh," I said. "Me neither."

He nodded, and I wasn't afraid anymore. But as soon as the fear was gone, I filled up with guilt. "Look at you," my brain said, "chatting with the kid who punched Sal!" My brain has a way of talking to me like that.

"I've got to go," I said, and I didn't let myself glance back until I got to the corner. When I did, the kid who punched Sal was gone. That was when I realized that he must live in the apartment over the garage, the one with dead plants on the fire escape and bedsheets hanging over the windows.

I'd forgotten all about the laughing man. His legs were sticking out from under the mailbox, and I was careful not to wake him.

When You Reach Me

REBECCA STEAD

Miranda's life is starting to unravel. Her best friend, Sal, gets punched by a kid on the street for what seems like no reason, and he shuts Miranda out of his life. Then the key Miranda's mum keeps hidden for emergencies is stolen, and a mysterious note arrives:

'I am coming to save your friend's life, and my own. I ask two favours. First, you must write me a letter.'

The notes keep coming, and whoever is leaving them knows things no one should know. Each message brings her closer to believing that only she can prevent a tragic death. Until the final note makes her think she's too late.

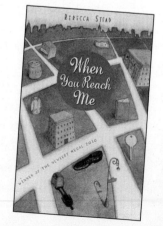

Winner of the John Newbery Medal 2010

Shortlisted for the Waterstone's Children's Book Prize

'Smart and mesmerising'
New York Times

9781849392129 £5.99